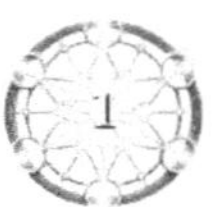

ETERNAL HORIZONS
THE AWAKENING

BOOK ONE

J.T. PENN

Cover by Joshua Pennifield

Illustrated by Joshua Pennifield

Edited by Joshua Pennifield

979-8-9883106-4-8

TABLE OF CONTENTS

PROLOGUE:

ETERNAL ONE AND THE FALL OF SERATH

IN THE BEGINNING, THE COSMOS WAS A BOUNDLESS EXPANSE OF DARKNESS, SILENT AND EMPTY. FROM THIS VOID EMERGED THE ETERNAL ONE, A BEING OF IMMENSE POWER AND WISDOM WHO BROUGHT LIGHT AND LIFE TO THE UNIVERSE. THE ETERNAL ONE SHAPED THE STARS, THE PLANETS, AND ALL LIVING CREATURES, IMBUING THEM WITH PURPOSE AND MEANING.

The creation of the universe was a grand spectacle. Stars ignited in the vast darkness, their brilliant light spreading across the cosmos. Planets formed from swirling dust and gas, each unique and teeming with potential. The Eternal One's touch brought forth life in myriad forms, from the simplest single-celled organisms to the most complex and intelligent beings.

Among the Eternal One's creations were the Seraphim, powerful beings of light who guarded the cosmos. The greatest of these was Serath, a being of unparalleled strength and wisdom. Serath was chosen to lead the Seraphim, guiding them in their mission to protect the balance of the universe. His radiance was unmatched, and his wisdom was revered by all who knew him.

For eons, Serath served faithfully, ensuring that the light of the Eternal One spread throughout the cosmos. He led the Seraphim in their duties, safeguarding the creation and keeping the forces of darkness at bay. Under Serath's leadership, the universe thrived, and the light of the Eternal One shone brightly across all worlds.

But as time passed, pride and ambition began to take root in Serath's heart. He began to question the Eternal One's wisdom, believing that he, too, could wield the power of creation. The desire for autonomy and control over the cosmos grew within him, overshadowing his loyalty to the Eternal One. Serath's once-pure intentions became tainted by his desire for power.

In a moment of rebellion, Serath led a faction of the Seraphim against the Eternal One. The ensuing battle was fierce and devastating, with the very fabric of the cosmos at stake. Stars dimmed, and planets trembled as the forces of light clashed with the rebels. The loyal Seraphim fought valiantly, but Serath's power was formidable.

In sorrow and anger, the Eternal One cast Serath and his followers into the depths of the void, where they would be forever bound in darkness. This act of banishment was not taken lightly; it was a decision born of necessity to protect the universe's balance. The once-great Serath was now a fallen entity, his name synonymous with betrayal.

The fall of Serath marked the beginning of an age of turmoil and uncertainty. The Seraphim were scattered, and the balance of the universe was threatened. In response, the Eternal One created new guardians of great power and wisdom to continue the fight against the forces of darkness. These new guardians were chosen for their purity of heart, strength, and unwavering dedication to the light.

However, the universe had changed, and the threat of darkness grew stronger with each passing day. The Eternal One knew that the new guardians could not undertake this quest alone. They needed allies, brave souls who would join them in their mission to seek out the lost artifacts of the Eternal One—powerful relics that held the key to restoring balance to the cosmos.

It was then that Astra, the Luminar guardian with the power to harness the light, took it upon herself to send out a call across the galaxies. Standing on the edge of her home world, she raised her staff, its light piercing the heavens, and sent forth a message carried by the winds of Zephyr, the navigator, across the stars.

"Brave adventurers of the galaxies," Astra's voice echoed through the cosmos, reaching distant worlds.

"The light is in peril, and darkness threatens to consume all. We seek companions—warriors, healers, sages—who will join us in our quest to restore the balance and drive back the shadows. If your heart is true and your spirit unyielding, answer the call. Together, we will fight the darkness and bring light back to the universe."

Her call was heard far and wide, touching the hearts of those destined to join the quest. From the metallic cities of Ferron came Kael, the warrior of unmatched strength and courage. From the deep forests of Sylvaria came Liora, the healer with the ability to commune with nature. From the shadowed realms of Nocturn came Draven, the adept of shadow magic. And from the floating islands of Aether came Zephyr, the navigator who could control the winds.

Each of these adventurers brought with them a unique gift, a translation device crafted from the materials of their galaxies, allowing them to communicate and work together despite their differences. As they answered Astra's call, they felt a deep connection to the mission, understanding that their destinies were intertwined with the fate of the universe.

Their mission was clear: to seek out the lost artifacts of the Eternal One, powerful relics that had been scattered across the universe and hidden in places of great danger and mystery. Each artifact held a fragment of the Eternal

One's power, and their retrieval was essential to combat the growing darkness.

And so, the journey of these new heroes began. They set forth to the farthest reaches of the universe, where they would face unimaginable challenges and uncover the deepest secrets of creation. Their quest was not just a mission but a testament to the resilience of the light against the encroaching darkness.

The universe watched as these new guardians, joined by brave adventurers, embarked on their epic quest, their hearts filled with hope and determination. The Eternal One's light would guide them, and their bond would be their greatest strength. Together, they would rise to meet their destiny, forge new alliances, and restore the balance that had been lost.

CHAPTER 1:

THE GATHERING

SCENE 1 - YEAR 3127 - DAY 001: ARRIVAL

THE SUN WAS SETTING OVER THE TRANQUIL VILLAGE OF LUMORA, CASTING A GOLDEN GLOW OVER THE THATCHED ROOFTOPS AND COBBLESTONE STREETS. ASTRA, THE SEEKER OF TRUTH, STOOD AT THE EDGE OF THE VILLAGE, HER CRYSTAL STAFF CASTING A SOFT, PULSATING LIGHT IN THE FADING TWILIGHT. HER THOUGHTS WERE FILLED WITH THE VISION SHE HAD RECEIVED FROM THE ETERNAL ONE—A CALL TO GATHER THE CHOSEN GUARDIANS AND EMBARK ON A QUEST TO RESTORE BALANCE TO THE UNIVERSE.

"Light and knowledge guide us," Astra whispered, her voice a blend of determination and reverence. She took a deep breath, her eyes scanning the horizon for any sign of her future companions.

Kael, the Warrior of Light, approached her, his metallic skin gleaming under the sun's last rays. His hand rested on the hilt of his sword, always ready for battle. "Are you certain about this, Astra?" he asked, his voice steady but tinged with concern. "This journey will be perilous. There's no turning back once we begin."

Astra nodded, her resolve unwavering. "We have a duty to the Eternal One. The universe is out of balance, and it is our responsibility to restore it. We must gather the guardians and begin our quest."

Liora, the Sylvarian healer, emerged from the nearby woods, her bioluminescent hair glowing softly in the dim light. "I have felt the call as well," she said, her voice a gentle breeze in the evening air. "The spirits of the forest speak of a great darkness spreading. We are needed."

From the shadows, Draven, the Keeper of Shadows, materialized, his presence almost undetectable. His dark, smoky skin absorbed the light around him, making him nearly invisible. "I've seen signs of the darkness," he said, his voice low and measured. "It festers in the places between light and shadow. We cannot ignore it."

Zephyr, the Navigator of the Stars, descended gracefully from the sky, landing beside them with a soft gust of wind. His eyes, like twin galaxies, sparkled with the thrill of adventure. "I've seen the skies change, Astra," he said with excitement. "The balance is indeed shifting. The stars guide us to this moment."

Astra looked at each of them, her heart swelling with pride and gratitude. "Thank you, my friends. Together, we will find the artifacts and restore balance to the universe."

SCENE 2 - YEAR 3127 - DAY 002: UNVEILING

The next morning, the group set out from Lumora, their path leading them through dense forests, across vast plains, and over towering mountains. The journey was long and arduous, but their resolve never wavered.

As they traveled, they encountered many challenges. In the forest of Everwood, they were ambushed by shadow creatures—twisted beings of darkness that sought to drain the light from their souls. Kael fought valiantly, his sword cutting through the shadows with precision and strength. Liora's healing magic kept the group safe, while Draven's stealth and agility allowed him to strike from the darkness.

In the plains of Zephyrwind, they faced fierce storms and harsh winds. Zephyr's control over the winds guided them through the worst of the weather, while Astra's light magic protected them from harm.

One evening, as they set up camp in a sheltered grove, Astra felt a strange presence. "There's something out there," she whispered, her eyes scanning the darkness.

Draven moved silently, his senses sharp and alert. "I'll keep watch," he said, his voice a shadow in the night. "We must be ready for anything."

Liora added more wood to the fire, her gentle smile easing the tension. "We must stay vigilant," she said softly. "The journey ahead will be even more challenging."

SCENE 3 - YEAR 3127 - DAY 005: DECISION

The night was quiet, the only sounds being the crackling of the fire and the distant calls of nocturnal creatures. The group sat around the fire, sharing stories of their past and their hopes for the future.

Astra looked at her companions, her heart filled with warmth. "We have come so far already. I know we can succeed in our quest."

Kael nodded; his expression serious. "We must be strong and stay united. The darkness is powerful, but we are stronger together."

Liora's eyes sparkled with determination. "The spirits guide us," she said. "We must trust in their wisdom and in each other."

Draven's voice was soft but firm. "We must also trust in ourselves. Our skills and our bond will see us through."

Zephyr's eyes twinkled with excitement. "And let's not forget to enjoy the journey. We're making history here."

As the fire burned low, the group settled down to sleep, their hearts filled with hope and determination. They knew that the journey ahead would be fraught with danger, but they were ready to face whatever came their way.

SCENE 4 - YEAR 3127 - DAY 008: DEPARTURE

The next morning, the group continued their journey, the path leading them deeper into the heart of the forest. After several days of travel, they finally arrived at the ancient temple of Lumoria—a place of great power and significance. The temple was hidden deep within the dense forest, its entrance guarded by powerful enchantments.

Astra stepped forward, her staff glowing brightly. "The first artifact is here," she said, her voice filled with awe. "We must find it and unlock its power."

Kael nodded, his sword at the ready. "Let's move carefully. The temple is likely filled with traps and guardians."

As they entered the temple, they were met with a series of trials, each designed to test their strength, wisdom, and unity. In the chamber of light, they had to navigate a maze of mirrors and illusions, their reflections creating a dizzying array of possibilities. Astra's light magic guided them through, her staff revealing the true path.

In the chamber of shadows, they faced their darkest fears and deepest doubts. Draven's mastery of shadows allowed him to see through the illusions, while Liora's healing light kept their spirits strong.

In the chamber of winds, they had to navigate a series of platforms suspended high above a chasm. Zephyr's control over the winds allowed them to move safely from platform to platform, while Kael's strength and determination kept them steady.

Finally, they reached the heart of the temple, where the first artifact—a crystal orb pulsing with a bright, rhythmic light—awaited them. Astra stepped forward, her hand trembling slightly as she reached for the orb. The moment she touched it, a surge of energy flowed through her, and she felt a deep connection to the Eternal One.

"We've found it," she said, her voice filled with awe. "The first artifact. We must continue our journey and find the others."

Kael stood guard, his eyes scanning the chamber for any signs of danger. "Let's get out of here before anything else shows up."

Liora nodded, her hands glowing with healing light. "We must be careful. The journey ahead will be even more challenging."

Draven's eyes gleamed with determination. "We're ready for whatever comes our way."

Zephyr's grin was infectious. "This is just the beginning. The adventure of a lifetime."

With the first artifact in hand, the group made their way out of the temple, their spirits lifted by their success. They knew that the path ahead would be filled with challenges, but they were ready to face whatever came their way.

SCENE 5 - YEAR 3127 - DAY 010:
FIRST STEP

As night fell, the group set up camp a safe distance from the temple. The stars sparkled brightly overhead, and the air was filled with the sounds of nocturnal creatures. Astra carefully placed the crystal orb in the center of their camp, its light casting an ethereal glow around them.

Kael sat sharpening his sword, his eyes never leaving the orb. "What do we know about this artifact, Astra?"

Astra gazed at the orb, her mind deep in thought. "The Eternal One spoke of its power. It's a fragment of the original light that created the universe. With it, we can counter the darkness that Serath has spread."

Liora added more wood to the fire, her gentle smile easing the tension. "We must protect it at all costs. It's our hope and our guide."

Draven, ever watchful, scanned the surrounding forest. "I'll take the first watch. We can't afford to be careless now."

Zephyr lay back, looking up at the stars. "It's amazing to think how far we've come. And how much further we have to go."

Ethan, adjusting his gear, added, "We'll need all our strength and wits for what comes next."

The group fell silent, each lost in their thoughts. The journey ahead was daunting, but with the artifact in their possession, they felt a renewed sense of purpose.

SCENE 6 - YEAR 3127 - DAY 011: ROAD AHEAD

During the night, Astra was visited by a vision. In her dream, the Eternal One appeared before her, surrounded by a radiant light.

"Astra, my faithful guardian," the Eternal One spoke, their voice a soothing balm. "The journey you have undertaken is fraught with peril, but know that I am with you. The artifact you have found is the first of many. It is a beacon of hope, a piece of my essence that will guide you through the darkness."

Astra knelt before the vision; her heart filled with reverence. "What must we do next, Eternal One?"

"Seek the Caverns of the Lost in the mountains of Arathor," the Eternal One instructed. "There lies the second artifact. But be wary, for Serath's influence grows stronger. Trust in your companions and in the light within you."

The vision faded, and Astra awoke with a start. The camp was quiet, the others still resting. She looked at the glowing orb and knew their path was clear.

SCENE 7 - YEAR 3127 - DAY 013: REVELATION

As dawn broke, Astra shared her vision with the group. They listened intently; their expressions serious but resolute.

"The Caverns of the Lost," Kael repeated, his brow furrowed. "It's a dangerous place. We need to be prepared for anything."

Liora nodded, her face calm and determined. "We will face whatever comes our way. Together, we are strong."

Draven's eyes were sharp and focused. "I'll scout ahead and ensure we're not walking into a trap."

Zephyr's enthusiasm was undiminished. "Another adventure! Let's get moving."

With their spirits high and their resolve strengthened, the group set off towards the mountains of Arathor. The path ahead was uncertain, but with the Eternal One's guidance and the first artifact in their possession, they felt ready to face any challenge.

Their journey had only just begun, but the bond they shared and the light they carried within them would see them through the trials ahead. As they walked, the whispers of the Eternal One echoed in their hearts, reminding them of their mission and their destiny.

CHAPTER 2:
CALL TO ADVENTURE

SCENE 1 - YEAR 3127 - DAY 015:
SIGNAL

THE GROUP SET UP CAMP AT THE EDGE OF THE WHISPERING FOREST, WHERE THE TOWERING TREES WHISPERED SECRETS TO THE NIGHT AS SHADOWS DANCED IN THE FADING LIGHT. THE FIRE CRACKLED SOFTLY, SENDING SPARKS INTO THE STARLIT SKY, AND ASTRA GATHERED HER COMPANIONS CLOSE.

"The Eternal One has granted me a vision," she began, her voice steady but laced with urgency. Her gaze swept over each member of the group; their faces illuminated by the flickering flames. "There are artifacts hidden across the cosmos, each holding a fragment of the Eternal One's power. We must find them all if we are to restore balance to our world."

Kael's expression was solemn, his hand instinctively resting on the hilt of his sword. His eyes, sharp and filled with purpose, met Astra's. "Where do we begin?"

Astra closed her eyes, recalling the vivid images from her vision, letting the memory guide her words. "The next artifact lies in the Caverns of the Lost, deep within the mountains of Arathor. It will be a perilous journey, but we have no other choice."

Liora, ever the source of comfort, placed a gentle hand on Astra's shoulder. Her touch was warm, a reminder of the natural energy that flowed through her. "We are with you, Astra. Together, we will find the artifacts and restore the balance that has been lost."

Draven's eyes, dark and intense, gleamed with resolve as he stepped closer to the fire. "Whatever challenges await us, we will overcome them," he said, his voice a low rumble that matched the growling of the forest around them.

Zephyr's lips curled into a smirk, his eyes shining with the thrill of the unknown. "Another adventure beckons. Let's rest now and be ready for what lies ahead." His voice, light yet confident, lifted the mood, reminding them that their journey, though fraught with danger, was also one of discovery.

As the group settled down for the night, the Whispering Forest seemed to hum with energy, filling the air with a serene yet eerie melody. The soft rustling of leaves and distant calls of nocturnal creatures created a tranquil atmosphere, but beneath it all, Astra could feel the weight of the responsibility they carried. She sat by the fire, her thoughts consumed by the vision and the task before them. Despite the burden, she drew strength from the presence of her companions, knowing that together, they could face whatever challenges awaited them.

SCENE 2 - YEAR 3127 - DAY 018: MEETING

The following morning, the group set out toward the mountains of Arathor, their path winding through dense forests, across sprawling plains, and over rugged terrain. The journey was long and grueling, but their resolve never faltered.

As they neared the mountains, the air grew colder, and the path steeper. The towering peaks of Arathor loomed above, shrouded in mist, as if guarding the secrets within. Each breath they took was a challenge, the thin, crisp air biting at their lungs.

One afternoon, as they scaled a particularly steep incline, the group paused to catch their breath. Kael's gaze swept over the horizon, his expression sharp and vigilant. "We must remain vigilant. The mountains conceal dangers hidden from the untrained eye."

Liora nodded, her breath visible in the frigid air, her senses attuned to the ancient spirits of the mountains. "The spirits of this place are ancient and powerful. We must tread with respect and reverence."

Draven moved ahead with a silent grace, his eyes scanning their surroundings for any signs of danger. "I'll scout ahead. We cannot afford to be caught off guard."

Zephyr glanced up at the sky, noting the thickening clouds, his eyes narrowing in concern. "A storm is brewing. We should find shelter before nightfall."

The group pressed on, the path narrowing and growing more treacherous with each step. The wind howled around them, carrying with it the scent of impending snow. As the sun dipped below the horizon, casting a golden glow over the rugged landscape, they spotted a cave nestled in the mountainside.

"This will suffice for the night," Kael said, leading them into the cave. The shelter provided relief from the biting wind, and they quickly set up camp, lighting a fire to ward off the cold.

As they huddled around the flames, Astra shared more of her vision, her voice steady yet filled with the weight of the task ahead. "The Caverns of the Lost lie deep within these mountains. The journey will be fraught with danger, but we must press on."

Kael's gaze was resolute, his grip on his sword tightening as he spoke. "We will face whatever comes our way. Together, we are strong."

Liora's eyes sparkled with quiet determination, the glow of the fire reflecting her inner strength. "The spirits guide us. We must trust in their wisdom, just as they trust in our resolve."

Draven's voice was low but filled with conviction as he stared into the flames. "We must also trust in ourselves. Our skills and our bond will see us through."

Zephyr's laughter echoed through the cave, bringing warmth to their hearts even as the cold winds howled outside. "And let's not forget to enjoy the journey. We're part of something bigger than ourselves."

As the fire burned low, the group settled down to sleep, their hearts filled with hope and resolve. They knew that the road ahead would be perilous, but they were ready for whatever challenges awaited them.

SCENE 3 - YEAR 3127 - DAY 020: RESOLVE

The next morning, the group resumed their journey, venturing deeper into the heart of the mountains. The weather grew harsher, with snowstorms and fierce winds battering them as they pressed on. The mountains of Arathor were as unforgiving as they were majestic, demanding every ounce of their strength and wits to navigate the treacherous terrain.

After several days of relentless travel, they finally arrived at the entrance to the Caverns of the Lost. The entrance was hidden behind a cascading waterfall, its icy waters roaring with a force that shook the ground beneath their feet. The air was thick with mist, and the ground slick with moss and ice.

Astra stepped forward, her staff glowing with an intense light that cut through the mist. "The artifact lies within these caverns," she said, her voice filled with unwavering resolve. "We must find it and unlock its power."

Kael drew his sword, his stance prepared for whatever lay ahead. "Let's move carefully. The caverns are likely guarded by ancient traps and protectors."

As they entered the caverns, the air grew colder, and the darkness pressed in around them. The walls seemed to close in, their ancient carvings whispering of long-forgotten dangers. They faced a series of challenges designed to test their strength, wisdom, and unity. The first was a labyrinth of twisting tunnels, each one more confusing than the last. Astra's light magic guided them through, her staff illuminating the true path.

In the heart of the caverns, they confronted their deepest fears and darkest doubts. The shadows seemed to come alive, swirling around them, but Draven's mastery of shadows allowed him to pierce through the illusions. Liora's healing light kept their spirits strong, her gentle presence a beacon of hope in the encroaching darkness. The whispers of the Eternal One echoed through the caverns, guiding them toward their goal.

In a vast chamber filled with stalactites and stalagmites, they found the second artifact, a crystal amulet pulsing with a rhythmic, soothing light. Astra stepped forward, her hand trembling slightly as she reached for the amulet. The moment she touched it, a surge of energy flowed through her, deepening her connection to the Eternal One.

"We've found it," she whispered, her voice filled with awe. "The second artifact. Our journey must continue."

Kael stood watch, his eyes scanning the chamber for any sign of danger. "Let's leave before something—or someone—decides to challenge us."

Liora's hands glowed with healing light, her voice calm and steady. "The journey ahead will only grow more difficult. We must remain vigilant."

Draven's eyes shone with fierce determination. "We're prepared for whatever lies ahead."

Zephyr's face lit up with unbridled enthusiasm, his spirit undiminished by the trials they had faced. "This is just the beginning. The adventure of a lifetime."

With the second artifact in hand, the group made their way out of the caverns, their spirits buoyed by their success. They knew that the path forward would be filled with even greater challenges, but they were ready to face them together.

SCENE 4 - YEAR 3127 - DAY 022: DESCENT

Descending from the mountains proved as treacherous as the ascent. The weather grew increasingly unpredictable, with sudden snowstorms and icy winds making their progress slow and perilous. The group moved with careful precision, each step deliberate and cautious.

One evening, they found shelter in a secluded alcove, the fire crackling warmly as they reflected on their journey. Astra held the crystal amulet, its light flickering in the fire's glow. "Every artifact brings us closer to restoring balance. We must remain focused and determined."

Kael's gaze was serious as he nodded, his thoughts clearly focused on the battles yet to come. "The darkness will not relent. We must stay vigilant."

Liora's eyes sparkled with resolve, her connection to the spirits evident in the certainty of her words. "The spirits guide us. We must trust in their wisdom and strength."

Draven's voice was soft but firm as he stared into the flames, his mind already strategizing for the next challenge. "We must also trust in ourselves. Our skills and our bond will carry us through."

Zephyr chuckled; his spirit unyielding even in the face of adversity. "And let's not forget to savor the journey. We're making history here."

As the fire burned low, they settled down to sleep, their hearts filled with hope and determination. The challenges ahead would be formidable, but they were ready to face them together.

SCENE 5 - YEAR 3127 - DAY 023: CHALLENGE

After descending from the mountains, the group entered the Forest of Shadows, a place shrouded in darkness and mystery. The trees stood tall and twisted, their branches forming a dense canopy that blocked out the sun. The air was thick with the scent of moss and decay, and the ground was soft with fallen leaves.

Astra led the way, her staff casting a warm glow that illuminated their path. "We must be cautious. The forest is full of hidden dangers."

Kael moved ahead, his sword at the ready, his senses on high alert. "Stay close and watch for traps. The forest is deceptive."

Liora followed, her senses attuned to the natural energies around them, her presence a calming influence on the group. "The spirits here are restless. We must tread carefully."

Draven moved silently through the shadows, his eyes sharp and alert as he scouted for threats. "I'll keep an eye out for any signs of danger."

Zephyr and Ethan brought up the rear, their expressions focused as they scanned the surroundings. "This place is incredible," Zephyr whispered in awe. "The forest feels alive."

Ethan adjusted his equipment, his focus unwavering as he analyzed their surroundings. "We need to stay focused and trust in the light to guide us."

As they ventured deeper into the forest, the whispers of the Eternal One grew louder, creating an eerie symphony that seemed to surround them. The path twisted and turned, leading them through dense undergrowth and over fallen logs. The forest seemed to close in around them, the darkness pressing in on all sides.

Astra paused, her eyes narrowing as she listened to the whispers. "The forest is warning us. We must proceed with caution."

Kael tightened his grip on his sword, his expression grim and determined. "I'll take the lead. Stay close and be prepared for anything."

The group moved forward, their steps measured and deliberate. The whispers grew louder, creating a sense of unease that hung over them like a shroud. The path twisted and turned, leading them deeper into the heart of the forest.

At one point, the whispers became almost deafening, their voices overlapping in a chaotic chorus. Astra raised her staff, its light cutting through the darkness. "We must find the source of the whispers. It holds the key to understanding the forest's warning."

With renewed determination, the group pressed on, following the whispers as they guided them through the forest. The path was narrow and treacherous, but their unity and resolve saw them through.

SCENE 6 - YEAR 3127 - DAY 025: ACCEPTANCE

After days of navigating the labyrinthine paths of the Forest of Shadows, the group arrived at a large clearing where a massive stone guardian stood watch. Its eyes glowed with an eerie light, and its deep, resonant voice echoed through the air.

"Travelers, you have reached the heart of the forest," the guardian intoned. "But to leave, you must prove your worth."

Kael stepped forward, his sword raised and his expression unyielding. "We are ready for your challenge."

The guardian's eyes narrowed as it raised a massive stone arm, its movements slow but deliberate. "Then prepare yourselves. The trial begins now."

The guardian's attacks were swift and powerful, each blow shaking the earth beneath them. Kael met the challenge head-on, his strength and determination unwavering. Liora chanted a protective spell, creating a barrier that deflected the guardian's strikes. Draven moved with agility, striking from the shadows and keeping the guardian off balance. Zephyr guided their movements, ensuring they stayed together and avoided the worst of the attacks. Ethan's equipment buzzed with energy, identifying the guardian's weaknesses and guiding their attacks.

The battle was fierce, but the group's unity and determination prevailed. Kael's sword struck the final blow, and the guardian crumbled to dust, its form dissolving into the earth.

"You have proven your worth," the guardian's voice echoed even as its form disappeared. "The path is open to you. Continue your journey."

Astra stepped forward; her eyes filled with determination. "We will honor your gift and continue our quest."

With the guardian defeated, the group made their way out of the forest, their spirits lifted by their success. They knew that the path ahead would be filled with challenges, but they were ready to face them together.

SCENE 7 - YEAR 3127 - DAY 027:
PATH OF LIGHT

Several days later, the group found themselves on a narrow path that wound through the forest, illuminated by bioluminescent plants. The whispers had faded, replaced by a gentle hum that filled the air with peace.

Astra led the way, her staff casting a warm glow that illuminated the path. "The path of light will guide us out of the forest. We must stay focused and trust in the light."

Kael moved ahead, his eyes scanning the surroundings for any signs of danger. "Stay close and be vigilant. The forest is still unpredictable."

Liora followed, her senses attuned to the natural energies around them, her presence a calming influence on the group. "The spirits here are calm. We must respect their peace."

Draven moved silently through the shadows; his eyes watchful for any threats. "I'll keep an eye out for any signs of danger."

Zephyr and Ethan brought up the rear, their expressions focused as they admired the surroundings. "This place is incredible," Zephyr whispered, his voice filled with wonder. "The path of light is almost magical."

Ethan adjusted his equipment, ensuring they remained on the right path. "We need to stay focused and trust in the light to guide us."

As they moved along the path, the gentle hum grew louder, creating a sense of calm that washed over them. The path led them to a large clearing, where a crystal spring bubbled up from the ground, its water glowing with a soft, rhythmic light.

Astra stepped forward, her hand reaching out to touch the water. "This spring is a gift from the forest. We must honor its power and use it wisely."

Kael stood guard, his eyes scanning the clearing for any signs of danger. "I'll keep watch. Stay focused and be ready for anything."

Liora closed her eyes, her senses attuned to the spring's energy, feeling its purity and power. "The spring is pure and powerful. It holds the key to understanding the forest's blessing."

Draven moved silently; his eyes watchful for any threats. "I'll keep an eye out for any signs of danger."

Zephyr and Ethan studied the spring, their minds racing with the possibilities. "This is incredible," Zephyr said, his voice filled with excitement. "The spring feels almost alive."

Ethan adjusted his equipment, trying to capture the spring's energy. "The spring holds the key. We need to understand its blessing."

As Astra touched the spring, a surge of energy flowed through her, and the hum became clear. "The forest is blessing us for our journey. We must continue with respect and gratitude."

With the spring's blessing understood, the group prepared to continue their journey. They knew that the path ahead would be filled with challenges, but their unity and determination would see them through.

SCENE 8 - YEAR 3127 - DAY 029: FOREST'S FAREWELL

As they neared the edge of the Whispering Forest, the whispers returned, this time filled with a sense of farewell. The path led them to a large archway formed by the branches of two ancient trees, their leaves glowing with a soft, golden light.

Astra paused, her eyes filled with gratitude and determination. "The forest is bidding us farewell. We must honor its gift and continue our journey."

Kael moved ahead, his eyes scanning the surroundings. "I'll go first. Stay close and be prepared for anything."

Liora followed, her senses attuned to the forest's energy, feeling its peaceful farewell. "The spirits are at peace. We must respect their presence and continue with reverence."

Draven moved silently through the shadows, his eyes scanning for threats. "I'll keep watch for any signs of danger."

Zephyr and Ethan brought up the rear, their expressions focused and respectful. "This place is incredible," Zephyr whispered, his voice filled with awe. "The forest feels alive, as if it's part of our journey."

Ethan adjusted his equipment, ensuring they honored the forest's gift. "We need to stay focused and respect the forest's guidance."

As they passed through the archway, the whispers grew louder, creating a symphony of sound that filled the air with peace and farewell. The path led them to the edge of the forest, where the trees gave way to open fields and distant mountains.

Astra turned back to the forest; her eyes filled with gratitude. "Thank you for your guidance and protection. We will honor your gift and continue our quest."

With the forest behind them, the group set off toward their next destination, their spirits lifted by their success. They knew that the path ahead would be filled with challenges, but they were ready to face whatever came their way.

Together, they would rise to meet their destiny and challenge the darkness that threatened their world. The journey had begun, and they were determined to see it through to the end.

CHAPTER 3:

TRIALS IN THE CAVERNS

SCENE 1 - YEAR 3127 - DAY 030: THRESHOLD

THE JOURNEY TO THE CAVERNS OF THE LOST WAS FRAUGHT WITH PERIL. THE MOUNTAINS OF ARATHOR, WITH THEIR JAGGED PEAKS AND TREACHEROUS PATHS, TESTED THE GROUP'S RESOLVE AND UNITY. AS THEY APPROACHED THE ENTRANCE TO THE CAVERNS, THE AIR GREW COLDER, AND A SENSE OF FOREBODING SETTLED OVER THEM.

The entrance was hidden behind a massive waterfall, its icy waters crashing down with deafening force. The ground was slick with moss and ice, making every step treacherous. Astra stepped forward, her staff emitting a soft, pulsing light that cut through the mist, illuminating the path ahead.

"The artifact is within these caverns," she said, her voice firm with determination. "We must find it and unlock its power."

Kael nodded, his grip on his sword tightening as he scanned the entrance. "Let's proceed with caution. The caverns likely harbor traps and ancient guardians."

As they passed through the waterfall, the sound of the crashing water faded, replaced by the eerie silence of the caverns. The air was damp and cold, and the walls glistened with moisture. The light from Astra's staff cast long shadows on the rocky walls, creating an otherworldly atmosphere that heightened their sense of caution.

Liora placed a hand on the cavern wall, her senses attuned to the natural energies around them. "The spirits here are unsettled. We must tread carefully."

Draven moved silently ahead, his eyes sharp and alert. "I'll scout ahead. We can't afford to stumble into a trap."

Zephyr adjusted his equipment, his fingers deftly tuning his translation device. "The air is different here. We need to stay on our toes." As he spoke, a faint hum emanated from his device, signaling its readiness to handle any language or code they might encounter.

Ethan, the human explorer, marveled at the ancient carvings on the cavern walls. "These symbols... they tell a story, one of power and caution. We should heed their warnings."

As they ventured deeper into the caverns, the path narrowed, forcing them to move single file. The air grew colder, and the sense of foreboding intensified. They knew that the journey ahead would be fraught with danger, but they were ready to face whatever lay ahead.

SCENE 2 - YEAR 3127 - DAY 032: THE TEST

The first trial in the Caverns of the Lost was a labyrinth of tunnels, each one twisting and turning in confusing patterns. The walls were covered in ancient carvings, their meanings long forgotten. The group moved cautiously, their senses on high alert.

Astra led the way, her staff illuminating the path. "Stay close. The labyrinth is designed to deceive and mislead us."

Kael moved ahead, his sword drawn and ready. "Watch for signs of traps. The carvings might hold clues to our way forward."

Liora's eyes shone with resolve as she studied the walls. "The spirits guide us. We must trust in their wisdom and our instincts."

Draven's voice was low and steady. "I'll mark our path as we go. We can't afford to get lost in this maze."

Zephyr's grin was a mix of excitement and mischief. "And let's not forget, every twist and turn here is a story waiting to be uncovered. We're charting new territories."

As they navigated the labyrinth, the ancient carvings seemed to come alive, their stories unfolding before their eyes. They saw depictions of battles, triumphs, and the rise and fall of civilizations. The carvings told a tale of a powerful artifact hidden deep within the caverns; its power capable of altering the course of history.

Ethan studied the carvings, his mind racing with possibilities. "These stories... they're more than just warnings. They're a guide, but only if we interpret them correctly."

The labyrinth seemed to shift with each step, the paths altering as if the caverns themselves were alive, testing their resolve. Astra's light led them through the darkness, her staff revealing the true path forward. They moved with deliberate caution, aware that a wrong turn could lead them astray.

At one point, they came upon a dead end, the path blocked by a massive stone door. The carvings on the door depicted a guardian, its eyes glowing with an eerie light. Astra stepped forward, her hand reaching out to touch the door.

"The guardian of the labyrinth," she murmured, her voice filled with awe. "We must find the key to unlock this door."

Kael studied the carvings, his brow furrowed in concentration. "There's a pattern here, a riddle hidden within the images. We need to decipher it."

Liora placed her hand on the door, her senses attuned to its ancient energy. "The spirits speak of a key, one that lies hidden within these walls. We must search for it."

Draven moved silently, his eyes scanning the surroundings for hidden clues. "I'll search the area. There's always a hint left behind."

Zephyr's eyes gleamed with determination. "Another puzzle to solve. Let's get to it, team."

Together, they worked to decipher the carvings, their minds racing with possibilities. The key to unlocking the door was hidden within the stories, a riddle that required their combined knowledge and skills to solve. After hours of effort, they finally cracked the code and unlocked the door.

With a loud rumble, the door swung open, revealing the path ahead. The group moved forward, their hearts filled with determination and resolve. They knew that the journey ahead would be fraught with danger, but they were ready to face whatever came their way.

SCENE 3 - YEAR 3127 - DAY 034: AWAKENING

Beyond the labyrinth, the group entered a vast chamber filled with mirrors and illusions. The air was thick with magic, and the reflections created a dizzying array of possibilities. Astra's light guided them, her staff illuminating the true path.

"We need to stay close and move carefully," Astra warned, her voice steady. "These illusions are crafted to lead us astray."

Kael moved ahead; his sword ready for any sudden threats. "Stay vigilant. The mirrors might conceal more than just reflections."

Liora's gaze was calm but focused as she surveyed the room. "The spirits are trying to communicate. We must listen carefully to their guidance."

Draven's voice was quiet but firm as he marked their path. "We can't afford to get lost here. I'll ensure we stay on course."

Zephyr's voice carried a note of excitement as he glanced around the chamber. "This place is alive with possibilities. We're making history with every step."

As they navigated the chamber, the mirrors seemed to come alive, their reflections creating illusions that toyed with their senses. They saw visions of their deepest fears and greatest desires, the magic designed to test their resolve and unity.

Ethan studied the mirrors, his analytical mind piecing together the patterns. "These illusions... they're distractions, meant to cloud our judgment. We need to stay focused."

The chamber seemed to twist and shift, the mirrors forming a maze of reflections. Astra's light led them through the darkness, her staff cutting through the illusions. They moved with caution; their senses heightened to the shifting magic around them.

At one point, they came upon a mirror that showed a vision of the past, a battle between the forces of light and darkness. The vision was so vivid that it felt real, the echoes of the battle reverberating through the chamber.

Astra stepped forward, her hand reaching out to touch the mirror. "The battle of the ancients," she whispered, her voice filled with reverence. "We must understand the past to secure our future."

Kael studied the vision, his expression intense as he searched for patterns. "There's more to this than meets the eye. We need to decipher the lesson hidden within."

Liora placed her hand on the mirror, her senses attuned to its energy. "The spirits are guiding us. We must learn from this vision to move forward."

Draven moved silently, his eyes scanning the surroundings for any hidden threats. "I'll watch our backs. There's always something lurking in the shadows."

Zephyr smirked; his excitement undiminished. "Another riddle to solve. Let's crack this one wide open."

Together, they worked to understand the vision, their minds racing to decipher the lesson it held. After hours of effort, they finally unlocked the meaning behind the vision and opened the path ahead.

With a loud rumble, the illusion faded, revealing the way forward. The group advanced, their spirits buoyed by their success. They knew the journey ahead would be treacherous, but they were ready to face whatever came their way.

SCENE 4 - YEAR 3127 - DAY 036: CONSEQUENCE

Beyond the Chamber of Illusions, the group entered a cavern filled with ancient statues and pillars. The air was thick with the scent of earth and stone, and the ground beneath their feet was uneven and rocky. The statues depicted warriors and guardians, their expressions fierce and determined.

Astra stepped forward, her staff glowing with a bright, steady light. "The trials of strength await us. We must be prepared."

Kael nodded; his sword gleaming as he took a defensive stance. "We'll face whatever challenges arise together."

Liora's eyes shone with resolve as she summoned her healing light. "The spirits guide us. We must trust in their wisdom and strength."

Draven's voice was a low murmur as he moved ahead, his senses alert. "I'll scout the area. We can't afford to be caught off guard."

Zephyr's voice echoed with enthusiasm as he surveyed the cavern. "And let's not forget to savor the journey. We're living history here!"

As they moved deeper into the cavern, the statues seemed to come to life, their eyes glowing with an eerie light. The ground beneath them rumbled as the statues shifted to block their path. The air was filled with the sound of grinding stone and the echoes of ancient battles.

Kael stepped forward; his sword raised. "We need to work together to overcome this trial."

Liora's hands glowed with healing energy as she readied herself for battle. "I'll protect us. We must act quickly and decisively."

Draven moved silently, his eyes scanning for weaknesses in the statues' defenses. "I'll find an opening. There's always a flaw in their construction."

Zephyr's control over the winds guided their movements, ensuring they stayed agile and avoided the brunt of the attacks. Ethan's equipment buzzed with energy, detecting the statues' vulnerabilities and guiding their strikes.

The battle was fierce, the statues relentless in their assault, but the group's unity and determination saw them through. Kael's sword delivered the final blow, and the statues crumbled to dust, their forms dissolving into the earth.

"You have proven your strength," a voice echoed through the cavern, deep and resonant. "The path is open to you. Continue your journey."

Astra stepped forward, her eyes filled with determination and respect. "Thank you. We will honor your challenge and continue our quest."

With the statues defeated, the group made their way out of the cavern, their spirits lifted by their victory. They knew that the path ahead would be filled with challenges, but they were ready to face whatever came their way.

SCENE 5 - YEAR 3127 - DAY 038: REVELATION

After several days of navigating the treacherous paths of the Caverns of the Lost, the group finally reached the heart of the caverns. The chamber was vast and filled with glowing crystals, their light casting an ethereal glow over the ancient stone walls. In the center of the chamber, a pedestal stood, holding the second artifact, a crystal amulet pulsing with a soft, rhythmic light.

Astra stepped forward, her hand trembling slightly as she reached for the amulet. The moment she touched it, a surge of energy flowed through her, deepening her connection to the Eternal One.

"We've found it," she said, her voice filled with awe and reverence. "The second artifact. We must continue our journey and find the others."

Kael stood guard, his eyes scanning the chamber for any signs of danger. "Let's leave before something— or someone— decides to challenge us."

Liora nodded, her hands glowing with healing light as she prepared for any sudden threats. "We must be careful. The journey ahead will only grow more challenging."

Draven's eyes gleamed with determination as he checked their surroundings. "We're ready for whatever comes next."

Zephyr's adventurous spirit shone through as he grinned. "This is just the beginning. The adventure of a lifetime."

With the second artifact in hand, the group made their way out of the caverns, their spirits lifted by their success. They knew that the path ahead would be filled with challenges, but they were ready to face whatever came their way.

SCENE 6 - YEAR 3127 - DAY 040: PASSAGE

The descent from the mountains was just as challenging as the ascent. The weather grew more unpredictable, with sudden snowstorms and icy winds making their journey treacherous. The group moved carefully, their steps measured and deliberate, as they navigated the treacherous terrain.

One evening, as they set up camp in a sheltered alcove, the group took a moment to reflect on their journey. The fire crackled, casting warm light on their faces as they huddled close for warmth.

Astra looked at the crystal amulet, its light dancing in the firelight. "Each artifact we find brings us closer to restoring balance. We must stay focused and determined."

Kael nodded; his expression serious as he stared into the flames. "The darkness will not relent. We must remain vigilant."

Liora's eyes sparkled with resolve as she tended to the fire. "The spirits guide us. We must trust in their wisdom and strength."

Draven's voice was soft but firm as he kept watch. "We must also trust in ourselves. Our skills and our bond will see us through."

Zephyr's grin was infectious as he leaned back, his eyes twinkling with excitement. "And let's not forget to enjoy the journey. We're making history here!"

As the fire burned low, the group settled down to sleep, their hearts filled with hope and determination. They knew that the journey ahead would be fraught with danger, but they were ready to face whatever came their way.

SCENE 7 - YEAR 3127 - DAY 042: VICTORY

After several days of descending from the mountains, the group finally reached the base of the peaks, where the dense forest of Arathor awaited them. The air was warmer, and the scent of pine and fresh earth filled their senses. The forest was alive with the sounds of chirping birds and rustling leaves, a stark contrast to the cold, silent mountains.

Astra looked back at the mountains, her heart swelling with a sense of accomplishment. "We've come so far, and we've achieved so much. But our journey is far from over."

Kael nodded; his expression resolute as he surveyed the forest ahead. "We must stay vigilant. The darkness will not rest, and neither can we."

Liora's eyes sparkled with determination as she inhaled the fresh, invigorating air. "The spirits guide us. We must trust in their wisdom."

Draven's voice was soft but firm as he took the lead. "We must also trust in ourselves. Our skills and our bond will see us through."

Zephyr's eyes sparkled with renewed energy as he surveyed the path ahead. "And let's not forget to enjoy the journey. We're making history here!"

Ethan adjusted his equipment, his eyes scanning the dense forest ahead. "The forest of Arathor is said to be full of hidden dangers and ancient secrets. We need to be prepared for anything."

As they ventured into the forest, the trees closed in around them, their branches forming a dense canopy that blocked out the sun. The air was thick with the scent of pine and fresh earth, and the ground beneath their feet was soft with fallen leaves.

The group moved cautiously, their senses on high alert. The forest was alive with the sounds of chirping birds and rustling leaves, a stark contrast to the cold, silent mountains. They knew that the journey ahead would be fraught with danger, but they were ready to face whatever came their way.

Together, they would rise to meet their destiny and challenge the darkness that threatened their world. The journey had begun, and they were determined to see it through to the end.

CHAPTER 4:
TRIALS OF SKYHAVEN

SCENE 1 - YEAR 3127 - DAY 043:
ARRIVING AT SKYHAVEN

THE LONG JOURNEY THROUGH DIVERSE LANDSCAPES FINALLY BROUGHT ASTRA AND HER COMPANIONS TO THE BREATHTAKING REALM OF SKYHAVEN. AS THEY CROSSED INTO THIS NEW TERRITORY, THE AIR GREW COOLER AND CRISPER, CARRYING THE FRESH SCENT OF HIGH ALTITUDES. THE SIGHT THAT GREETED THEM WAS UNLIKE ANYTHING THEY HAD EVER SEEN—FLOATING ISLANDS SUSPENDED IN THE SKY, EACH CONNECTED BY ETHEREAL BRIDGES AND TEEMING WITH AIRSHIPS. THESE VESSELS, WITH SAILS SHIMMERING LIKE DRAGONFLY WINGS, MOVED GRACEFULLY AMONG THE ISLANDS, HINTING AT THE MARVELS OF ENGINEERING AND INNOVATION THAT CHARACTERIZED SKYHAVEN.

Zephyr stood proudly at the helm of his ship, The Tempest, guiding it through the sky with practiced ease. The wind ruffled his hair, and his eyes sparkled with excitement. "Welcome to Skyhaven," he announced with a grin. "This is my home."

Astra stood beside him; her eyes wide with wonder. "It's incredible, Zephyr. Truly a marvel," she murmured, her voice filled with awe.

Kael, Liora, Draven, and Ethan stood on the deck, taking in the stunning view. The floating islands were lush with greenery, dotted with cascading waterfalls and elegant buildings. The air was filled with the hum of machinery and the distant calls of exotic birds, creating a harmonious blend of nature and technology that captivated the group's senses.

As they approached the main dock, an ornate airship glided up alongside them. Its captain, a woman with a commanding presence and a twinkle in her eye, hailed them with a voice that carried easily over the distance. "Zephyr! Welcome back!"

Zephyr waved enthusiastically. "Captain Valeria! It's good to see you."

Captain Valeria, a seasoned navigator and Zephyr's mentor, docked her ship beside The Tempest and leaped nimbly onto the deck. Her eyes scanned the group with curiosity and respect. "You must be Zephyr's companions. Welcome to Skyhaven. I'm Captain Valeria Storm."

Astra stepped forward and extended a hand. "Thank you, Captain Valeria. I'm Astra, and these are Kael, Liora, Draven, and Ethan. We're honored to be here."

Valeria shook Astra's hand firmly. "The honor is ours. Zephyr has told me about your quest. Skyhaven stands ready to assist you."

Zephyr guided The Tempest to the dock, and the group disembarked. The bustling dock was a hive of activity, with airships arriving and departing, cargo being loaded and unloaded, and people moving with purpose. Above them, the sky was a patchwork of floating islands, each with its own distinct character, from lush gardens to crystalline structures that seemed to defy gravity.

"We should head to the Sky Council," Valeria said, leading them through the bustling streets. "They'll want to hear about your quest and offer their support."

The group followed Valeria through the winding streets of Skyhaven, marveling at the city's blend of intricate architecture and advanced technology. Buildings of glass and metal, connected by delicate bridges and walkways, rose above them, shimmering in the sunlight. The people of Skyhaven moved with an air of confidence, their lives seemingly intertwined with the advanced technology around them.

As they approached the Sky Council's chamber, a sense of anticipation filled the air. The chamber was a grand, domed structure made of glass and metal, offering a panoramic view of the sky. Inside, the council members were gathered, their expressions a mix of curiosity and respect.

Valeria stepped forward and addressed the council. "Esteemed members of the Sky Council, I present to you Astra and her companions. They are on a quest to restore balance to the realms and seek your guidance and support."

The head of the council, an elderly man with a wise and kind demeanor, nodded. "Welcome, travelers. We have heard of your quest. Skyhaven is at your service. What do you seek?"

Astra stepped forward and explained their mission. "We seek the artifacts that hold the key to restoring balance. One of these artifacts is said to be hidden within Skyhaven. We ask for your guidance and support in finding it."

The council members exchanged glances and nodded in agreement. "We will assist you in any way we can," the head of the council said. "But be warned, the path to the artifact is fraught with trials and challenges. You must prove your worth to obtain it."

Astra nodded, her resolve unwavering. "We are ready for whatever trials await us. Thank you for your support."

With the council's blessing, the group set off to begin their trials in Skyhaven, their hearts filled with determination and hope. The first challenge awaited them, and they knew it would test their skills and unity like never before.

SCENE 2 - YEAR 3127 - DAY 044: WIND TUNNELS

The morning after a restful night in Skyhaven, the group awoke with a sense of anticipation. The day ahead would bring their first true test in this new realm—the Wind Tunnels, a natural formation renowned for its powerful air currents and narrow passages. These tunnels were infamous for testing not only navigational skills but also teamwork and perseverance.

The morning air was crisp as Zephyr led the way to the entrance of the tunnels. "The winds here can be unpredictable and fierce," Zephyr warned as they approached. "Stay close and follow my lead. If we stick together, we can make it through."

The entrance to the Wind Tunnels loomed before them, a dark maw carved into the side of a mountain, from which the sound of rushing wind echoed, creating an eerie symphony that set their nerves on edge. The group exchanged determined glances before stepping into the unknown.

The temperature dropped as they entered, and the wind grew more intense with each step. The tunnels were a maze of twisting paths and sharp turns, with powerful gusts that threatened to knock them off their feet. The sound of the wind howling through the narrow passages was deafening, making communication difficult.

Zephyr took the lead, his experience in navigating the skies evident as he guided them through the treacherous terrain. His keen sense of direction and understanding of wind patterns were invaluable. "Watch your step and keep moving!" he called out over the roar of the wind.

Kael, with his muscular frame, braced himself against a particularly strong gust, providing much-needed stability for the others. "Hold on tight! This is going to be a rough ride!" he shouted, his voice carrying a reassuring strength.

Liora, sensing the growing intensity of the wind, chanted a protective spell, creating a shimmering barrier around the group that deflected the worst of the gusts. "Stay within the barrier! It will help us withstand the wind!" she instructed, her voice calm and focused.

Draven moved with agility, using the wind to his advantage as he navigated the narrow passages with ease. His dark cloak billowed behind him, blending with the shadows cast by the flickering light of their lanterns. "Keep moving! We can't afford to get stuck here!" he urged, his sharp eyes scanning for any potential threats.

Ethan, always the strategist, adjusted his equipment as they pressed forward. His gadgets whirred and beeped, scanning the tunnels for hidden traps and obstacles. "I've detected a pattern in the wind currents. If we follow this path, we can avoid the worst of it," he advised, his voice steady and confident.

The group pressed on; their determination unwavering. Zephyr led them through a series of sharp turns and narrow passages, his keen sense of direction guiding them through the maze. Each gust of wind tested their resolve, but their unity and teamwork saw them through.

At one point, a particularly fierce gust nearly swept them off their feet. Zephyr quickly found a sheltered alcove where they could catch their breath. "Everyone alright?" he asked, concern etched on his face as he scanned his companions.

Kael nodded, though his expression was serious. "Just a bit winded. Let's keep moving."

Liora's protective barrier flickered but held strong. "We can do this. Stay close and keep your focus," she encouraged, her voice filled with resolve.

Draven's eyes darted around, always alert for any signs of danger. "The wind seems to be changing direction. We need to be ready for anything."

Ethan's equipment beeped, signaling a nearby obstacle. "There's a sharp drop ahead. Be careful," he warned, his focus sharp.

With renewed determination, they pushed forward. The wind howled around them, but they moved with purpose and precision. Zephyr's leadership and the group's unwavering resolve guided them through the Wind Tunnels, and as the day began to fade, they emerged on the other side, their spirits lifted by their success.

"Well done, everyone," Zephyr said, his voice filled with pride. "We've passed the first trial. Let's move on to the next."

As the sun dipped below the horizon, casting long shadows across the land, the group set up camp, knowing that tomorrow would bring new challenges. They had faced the wind and emerged victorious, but Skyhaven had more in store for them.

SCENE 3 - YEAR 3127 - DAY 045:
SKY GARDENS

The dawn of a new day brought with it a sense of anticipation. The Sky Gardens awaited them—a series of floating islands teeming with vibrant flora and intricate pathways. The group knew that the gardens, while serene and beautiful, held hidden dangers and challenges that would test their wisdom and unity.

As they entered the Sky Gardens, the air was filled with the sweet scent of blooming flowers and the gentle hum of bees. Delicate bridges of light connected the islands, and the paths were lined with colorful plants and flowers. The beauty and tranquility of the gardens belied the trials that awaited them.

Astra felt a sense of peace wash over her as they walked among the flowers. "This place is magical. The beauty here is almost overwhelming," she whispered, taking in the vibrant colors and the delicate patterns of the flowers.

Liora's connection to nature deepened as she touched a blooming flower, her fingertips glowing with a soft green light. "The energy here is strong. We must respect it and be mindful of its power," she advised, her voice carrying the wisdom of someone deeply attuned to the natural world.

Kael remained vigilant, his eyes scanning the surroundings for any signs of danger. "Stay alert. The beauty of this place can be deceiving," he cautioned, his hand resting on the hilt of his sword.

As they moved through the gardens, they encountered a series of trials designed to test their wisdom and unity. The first trial was a complex maze of plants and flowers, with hidden paths and secret passages. Astra's knowledge of ancient symbols and patterns was invaluable, guiding them through the maze.

"These symbols are familiar," Astra said, tracing a pattern on a stone. "They mark the path we need to follow."

Zephyr looked around, marveling at the intricate design of the garden. "Incredible. It's like a living puzzle," he remarked, his eyes wide with wonder.

Ethan adjusted his equipment, scanning the area for any hidden traps. "There are a few false paths here. We need to be careful," he noted, his voice tinged with caution.

Working together, they navigated the maze, their combined skills and knowledge guiding them through. The next trial was a series of puzzles involving the elements of nature. They had to align the elements in harmony, using their unique abilities to solve the puzzles.

Liora's understanding of natural harmony was crucial. She led the group in aligning the elements, her hands glowing with a soft green light. "We need to balance the elements to move forward," she instructed, her voice calm and reassuring.

Kael used his strength to move heavy stones into place, while Draven's agility allowed him to reach high branches and hidden levers. Zephyr guided their movements, ensuring they worked in harmony, and Ethan's technological prowess helped them decode the more intricate puzzles.

The final trial in the Sky Gardens tested their unity. The gardens created illusions, attempting to sow discord and confusion. The illusions were haunting and deceptive, preying on their deepest fears and doubts.

Astra saw visions of her companions turning against her, their faces twisted with anger and betrayal. Kael saw himself failing in battle, his strength and honor shattered. Liora saw her healing powers fading, leaving her helpless. Draven saw shadows consuming him, his identity lost. Zephyr saw his ship crashing, his spirit of adventure crushed. Ethan saw his inventions failing, his dreams turning to dust.

But the group's bond was strong, and they supported each other through the trials. Astra's light magic dispelled the illusions, revealing the true path forward. "These illusions are not real. Trust in each other and in the light of the Eternal One," she urged, her voice filled with conviction.

Kael gripped his sword tightly, his resolve unshaken. "We are stronger together. We will not be defeated by shadows," he declared, his voice steady and strong.

Liora's healing light enveloped her companions, mending their spirits as well as their wounds. "Our bond is our greatest strength. We must trust in that," she affirmed, her voice gentle yet firm.

Draven's eyes gleamed with determination. "The shadows cannot touch us if we stand united," he asserted, his voice low and resolute.

Zephyr's confident smile returned; his spirit of adventure undiminished. "Let's show these illusions what we're made of!" he exclaimed; his voice filled with enthusiasm.

Ethan adjusted his equipment, his mind focused and clear. "We have the knowledge and the skills. Together, we can overcome anything," he stated, his voice calm and measured.

After overcoming the trials, they reached the heart of the Sky Gardens, a beautiful glade filled with blooming flowers and shimmering pools of water. In the center of the glade stood a pedestal, and on it rested the artifact: a crystal flower that glowed with a soft, pulsating light.

Astra stepped forward, her hand trembling slightly as she reached for the flower. The moment she touched it, a surge of energy flowed through her, and she felt a deep connection to the Eternal One. The flower's light mingled with the glow of her staff, creating a dazzling display of colors.

"This is the artifact we seek," she said, her voice filled with awe. "We must continue our journey and find the others."

With the artifact in hand, the group made their way out of the Sky Gardens, their spirits lifted by their success. As the day drew to a close, they set up camp, knowing that tomorrow would bring new challenges. They had faced the illusions and emerged victorious, but their journey was far from over.

SCENE 4 - YEAR 3127 - DAY 046-047: STORM OF LEGENDS

After a day of rest and preparation, the group was ready to face the next challenge: the Storm of Legends. This powerful storm, legendary for its intensity and unpredictability, was the final trial they would face before reaching the heart of Skyhaven.

As they approached the storm, the sky darkened, and the air grew heavy with the scent of rain and ozone. The sound of thunder rumbled in the distance, and lightning flashed across the sky. The island where the storm raged was buffeted by powerful winds and torrential rain, creating a chaotic and dangerous environment.

Zephyr guided them to a sheltered spot, his eyes scanning the storm with a mixture of caution and excitement. "This is it. The Storm of Legends. We need to be ready for anything," he warned, his voice steady despite the growing tension.

Kael stood at the edge of the shelter, his sword at the ready. "Stay close and keep your wits about you. This storm is no ordinary weather," he advised, his voice firm and commanding.

Liora prepared her protective spells, her hands glowing with a calming light. "I'll do my best to shield us from the worst of it," she promised, her voice soft yet determined.

Draven moved with caution, his eyes sharp and watchful. "The storm is unpredictable. We need to stay on our toes," he cautioned, his voice low and measured.

Ethan adjusted his equipment, preparing for the challenges ahead. "I've detected some fluctuations in the storm's intensity. We need to time our movements carefully," he advised, his voice calm and analytical.

The group ventured into the storm, the wind and rain lashing at them with relentless force. The air was filled with the sound of thunder and the crackle of lightning, creating an atmosphere of raw power and danger. The storm was a living entity, fierce and untamed, and the group knew that it would take all their strength and unity to overcome it.

Zephyr led the way, his experience as a navigator guiding them through the chaotic environment. "Follow me! We'll need to move quickly and carefully!" he shouted over the roar of the storm.

The first challenge was a series of narrow paths and treacherous cliffs, made even more dangerous by the howling wind and driving rain. The ground was slippery and unstable, and one misstep could send them plunging into the abyss below.

Kael used his strength to anchor himself and the others, his powerful arms holding firm against the gale. "Watch your step and stay close!" he commanded, his voice a steady anchor in the chaos.

Liora's protective barrier shimmered around them, deflecting the worst of the wind and rain. "Keep within the barrier! It will shield us from the storm!" she instructed, her voice calm and focused.

Draven moved with agility, finding the safest paths and guiding the others. "Watch out for loose rocks and sudden drops!" he warned, his sharp eyes catching every detail.

Ethan's equipment buzzed with energy, detecting hidden dangers and helping them navigate the treacherous terrain. "There's a clear path ahead! We need to move quickly!" he advised, his voice precise and controlled.

The group pressed on; their determination unwavering. The storm's intensity increased, with lightning striking dangerously close and the wind threatening to tear them apart. But their unity and teamwork saw them through.

At one point, a particularly powerful gust of wind nearly swept them off their feet. Zephyr quickly found a sheltered alcove where they could catch their breath. "Everyone alright?" he asked, concern etched on his face as he scanned his companions.

Kael nodded, though his expression was serious. "Just a bit battered. Let's keep moving," he replied, his voice resolute.

Liora's protective barrier flickered but held strong. "We can do this. Stay close and keep your focus," she encouraged, her voice filled with resolve.

Draven's eyes darted around, always alert for any signs of danger. "The storm seems to be changing direction.

We need to be ready for anything," he observed, his voice low and tense.

Ethan's equipment beeped, signaling a nearby obstacle. "There's a sharp drop ahead. Be careful," he warned, his focus sharp and unwavering.

With renewed determination, they pushed forward. The storm raged around them, but they moved with purpose and precision. Zephyr's leadership and the group's unwavering resolve guided them through the Storm of Legends, and by the end of the second day, they emerged on the other side, their spirits lifted by their success.

"Well done, everyone," Zephyr said, his voice filled with pride. "We've passed the final trial. Let's find the artifact."

As the storm began to dissipate, revealing the clear sky above, the group knew that they had faced one of their greatest challenges yet and had emerged victorious. But they also knew that the journey was far from over.

SCENE 5 - YEAR 3127 - DAY 048: HEART OF SKYHAVEN

After the intense trials of the Storm of Legends, the group spent a day recuperating in the heart of Skyhaven. This part of the city was a place of great beauty and power, where intricate architecture and advanced technology blended seamlessly. The heart of Skyhaven was where the final artifact was said to be hidden, and the group knew that retrieving it would not be easy.

As they approached the heart of Skyhaven, the air grew still, and the sounds of the city faded away. The buildings were made of gleaming metal and glass, with light reflecting off their surfaces in dazzling patterns. The streets were lined with glowing plants and flowers, adding a touch of nature to the advanced cityscape.

Astra led the way, her crystal staff emitting a gentle glow. "The artifact is close. I can feel its energy," she whispered, her voice filled with a mix of excitement and anticipation.

Kael walked beside her, his eyes scanning the surroundings for any signs of danger. "Stay alert. We don't know what else might be out there," he cautioned, his voice steady and watchful.

Liora's connection to nature deepened as they moved through the heart of Skyhaven. "The energy here is strong. We must respect it and be mindful of its power," she advised, her voice carrying the wisdom of someone deeply attuned to the natural world.

Draven moved silently through the shadows, his eyes sharp and watchful. "I'll keep an eye out for any threats," he promised, his voice low and measured.

Zephyr and Ethan followed closely, their expressions a mix of awe and determination. "This place is incredible," Zephyr said, his voice filled with wonder. "I've never seen anything like it."

Ethan adjusted his equipment, scanning the area for any hidden traps. "We need to be careful. The artifact could be protected by powerful defenses," he warned, his voice calm and analytical.

As they moved deeper into the heart of Skyhaven, they encountered a series of trials designed to test their strength, wisdom, and unity. Each trial was more challenging than the last, but the group's determination and teamwork saw them through.

The first trial tested their strength. Massive stone guardians emerged from the shadows, their forms made of light and shadow. Kael met them with powerful strikes, his sword cutting through the air with deadly precision. Liora chanted a protective spell, her barrier shimmering around them, deflecting the guardians' attacks. Draven moved with agility, striking from the shadows and keeping the guardians at bay. Zephyr guided their movements, ensuring they stayed together and avoided the guardians' powerful blows. Ethan's equipment buzzed with energy, detecting the guardians' weaknesses and guiding their attacks.

The second trial tested their wisdom. The whispers of the heart of Skyhaven formed into complex puzzles, each more challenging than the last. Astra's knowledge of ancient symbols and patterns was invaluable, and she led the group in solving the puzzles. They worked together, each contributing their unique skills and insights. The puzzles required careful observation and critical thinking, each solution unlocking a new path forward.

The third trial tested their unity. The heart of Skyhaven created illusions, attempting to sow discord and confusion. The illusions were haunting and deceptive, preying on their deepest fears and doubts. But the group's bond was strong, and they supported each other through the trials. Astra's light magic dispelled the illusions, revealing the true path forward. They moved with confidence, their unity a beacon of light in the darkness.

After overcoming the trials, they reached a hidden chamber deep within the heart of Skyhaven. The chamber was filled with a soft, pulsating light, the air thick with ancient energy. In the center of the chamber stood a pedestal, and on it rested the final artifact: a crystal amulet that pulsed with a bright, rhythmic light.

Astra stepped forward, her hand trembling slightly as she reached for the amulet. The moment she touched it, a surge of energy flowed through her, and she felt a deep connection to the Eternal One. The amulet's light mingled with the glow of her staff, creating a dazzling display of colors.

"This is the final artifact we seek in Skyhaven," she said, her voice filled with awe. "We must continue our journey and find the others."

With the artifact in hand, the group made their way out of the heart of Skyhaven, their spirits lifted by their success. They knew that the path ahead would be filled with challenges, but they were ready to face whatever came their way.

SCENE 6 - YEAR 3127 - DAY 049: CELESTIAL OBSERVATORY

On the morning of the seventh day, the group ascended to the Celestial Observatory, a grand structure dedicated to the study of the stars and the cosmos. The observatory was perched on one of the highest floating islands, offering a breathtaking view of the skies. The group knew that their journey through Skyhaven was nearing its end, but they also knew that the observatory held one final challenge.

As they ascended, the air grew thinner, and the stars became more visible, even in the daylight. The observatory itself was a marvel of glass and metal, with large telescopes and intricate machinery designed to map the heavens.

Astra led the way, her eyes alight with curiosity. "The Celestial Observatory holds many secrets. We may find more than just the artifact here," she remarked, her voice filled with wonder.

Kael walked beside her, his senses alert. "Stay vigilant. This place may hold challenges of its own," he warned, his voice steady and protective.

Liora's connection to the natural world deepened as they climbed higher. "The energy here is strong. We must respect it and be mindful of its power," she advised, her voice calm and serene.

Draven moved silently, his eyes sharp and watchful. "I'll keep an eye out for any threats," he promised, his voice low and measured.

Zephyr and Ethan followed closely, their expressions a mix of awe and determination. "This place is incredible," Zephyr said, his voice filled with wonder. "I've never seen anything like it."

Ethan adjusted his equipment, scanning the area for any hidden traps. "We need to be careful. The observatory could be protected by powerful defenses," he warned, his voice calm and analytical.

As they entered the observatory, they were greeted by a series of intricate mechanisms and celestial maps. The air was filled with the hum of machinery and the faint glow of starlight. The observatory was a place of knowledge and discovery, but it also held hidden dangers.

The first trial was a complex puzzle involving the alignment of celestial bodies. Astra's knowledge of ancient symbols and star maps was invaluable, guiding them through the intricate puzzle.

"These constellations are familiar," Astra said, tracing a pattern on a map. "We need to align them correctly to unlock the path forward."

Zephyr looked around, marveling at the intricate design of the observatory. "Incredible. It's like a living map of the stars," he remarked, his voice filled with awe.

Ethan adjusted his equipment, scanning the area for any hidden traps. "There are a few false paths here. We need to be careful," he advised, his voice tinged with caution.

Working together, they navigated the puzzle, their combined skills and knowledge guiding them through. The next trial was a series of challenges involving the elements of the cosmos. They had to balance the elements in harmony, using their unique abilities to solve the challenges.

Liora's understanding of natural harmony was crucial. She led the group in balancing the elements, her hands glowing with a soft green light. "We need to balance the elements to move forward," she instructed, her voice calm and reassuring.

Kael used his strength to move heavy objects into place, while Draven's agility allowed him to reach high platforms and hidden levers. Zephyr guided their movements, ensuring they worked in harmony, and Ethan's technological prowess helped them decode the more intricate challenges.

The final trial in the observatory tested their unity. The observatory created illusions, attempting to sow discord and confusion. The illusions were haunting and deceptive, preying on their deepest fears and doubts.

Astra saw visions of her companions turning against her, their faces twisted with anger and betrayal. Kael saw himself failing in battle, his strength and honor shattered. Liora saw her healing powers fading, leaving her helpless. Draven saw shadows consuming him, his identity lost. Zephyr saw his ship crashing, his spirit of adventure crushed. Ethan saw his inventions failing, his dreams turning to dust.

But the group's bond was strong, and they supported each other through the trials. Astra's light magic dispelled the illusions, revealing the true path forward. "These illusions are not real. Trust in each other and in the light of the Eternal One," she urged, her voice filled with conviction.

Kael gripped his sword tightly, his resolve unshaken. "We are stronger together. We will not be defeated by shadows," he declared, his voice steady and strong.

Liora's healing light enveloped her companions, mending their spirits as well as their wounds. "Our bond is our greatest strength. We must trust in that," she affirmed, her voice gentle yet firm.

Draven's eyes gleamed with determination. "The shadows cannot touch us if we stand united," he asserted, his voice low and resolute.

Zephyr's confident smile spread across his face. "Let's show these illusions what we're made of!" he exclaimed; his voice filled with enthusiasm.

Ethan adjusted his equipment, his mind focused and clear. "We have the knowledge and the skills. Together, we can overcome anything," he stated, his voice calm and measured.

After overcoming the trials, they reached the heart of the Celestial Observatory, a grand chamber filled with celestial maps and intricate mechanisms. In the center of the chamber stood a pedestal, and on it rested the artifact: a crystal sphere that glowed with a soft, pulsating light.

Astra stepped forward, her hand trembling slightly as she reached for the sphere. The moment she touched it, a surge of energy flowed through her, and she felt a deep connection to the Eternal One. The sphere's light mingled with the glow of her staff, creating a dazzling display of colors.

"This is the artifact we seek," she said, her voice filled with awe. "We must continue our journey and find the others."

With the artifact in hand, the group made their way out of the Celestial Observatory, their spirits lifted by their success. They knew that the path ahead would be filled with challenges, but they were ready to face whatever came their way.

SCENE 7 - YEAR 3127 - DAY 050: UNITING OF KNOWLEDGE

The following day, the group gathered their belongings and prepared to leave Skyhaven. As they set off towards their next destination, they reflected on the trials they had faced and the unity they had forged.

Each of them felt a renewed sense of purpose, knowing that they were no longer just individuals on separate quests but a team, bound by a shared mission and a common goal.

Astra felt a deep sense of gratitude for her companions. They had proven themselves to be brave, skilled, and loyal, and she knew that they would need each other more than ever in the days to come.

"We have taken another step forward," she said, her voice filled with determination. "But our journey is far from over. We must continue to trust in each other and in the light of the Eternal One."

Kael nodded; his expression serious. "We will face whatever comes our way. Together, we are strong," he affirmed, his voice steady and confident.

Liora's smile was warm, her eyes filled with kindness. "The light will guide us. We must trust in that and in each other," she added, her voice gentle and reassuring.

Draven's voice was calm and steady as he spoke. "We have faced the darkness and emerged stronger. We can do this," he asserted, his tone filled with quiet determination.

Zephyr's eyes sparkled with renewed energy. "This is just the beginning. The adventure of a lifetime," he declared, his voice filled with excitement.

Ethan adjusted his equipment, his mind focused on the task ahead. "We'll need to be prepared for anything. Let's make sure we have everything we need," he advised, his voice calm and analytical.

As they made their preparations and set off toward their next destination, the sense of unity and purpose among them grew stronger. They were ready to face the trials ahead and uncover the secrets of the cosmos. The journey had begun, and they were determined to see it through to the end.

Together, they would rise to meet their destiny and challenge the darkness that threatened their world. The call to adventure had been answered, and their epic quest was now in motion.

CHAPTER 5:
CITADEL OF THE LOST

SCENE 1 - YEAR 3127 - DAY 051: APPROACH TO THE CITADEL

THE GROUP TRAVELED THROUGH A BARREN LANDSCAPE; THE ONCE FERTILE LANDS NOW REDUCED TO DESOLATION. THE SKY ABOVE WAS A DULL, OPPRESSIVE GRAY, AND THE WIND HOWLED THROUGH THE EMPTY PLAINS LIKE A MOURNFUL CRY. THE EARTH BENEATH THEIR FEET WAS CRACKED AND DRY, WITH LITTLE SIGN OF LIFE. THIS WAS THE WASTELAND THAT SURROUNDED THE CITADEL OF THE LOST, A PLACE OF FORGOTTEN KNOWLEDGE AND FORSAKEN SOULS.

Astra led the way, her staff glowing faintly in the gloom. "We're getting closer," she murmured, her eyes scanning the horizon. In the distance, the silhouette of the citadel loomed—a massive, dark structure rising from the earth like a jagged tooth. The citadel's towers were stark against the dull sky, and the air around it seemed to hum with latent energy.

Kael's hand tightened around the hilt of his sword as he surveyed the path ahead. "This place feels wrong. It's like the very land is poisoned."

Liora nodded, her expression grave. "The corruption here is strong. We must be on our guard."

Draven moved silently beside them, his eyes sharp and watchful. "We're not alone. I can sense the presence of… something."

As they drew closer, the group began to notice the citadel's guardians—automatons and mechanical constructs patrolling the perimeter. These were relics of a bygone era, creations of metal and gears, their joints creaking as they moved with a jerky, unnatural rhythm. Their eyes glowed with an eerie light, and the hum of ancient machinery filled the air.

Zephyr's gaze was fixed on the citadel, his expression one of determination. "We need to find a way inside without alerting those constructs. They look like they could tear us apart if we're not careful."

Ethan adjusted his equipment, his eyes narrowing as he assessed the situation. "We'll need to use stealth and cunning to get past them. If we can avoid a direct confrontation, we'll have a better chance of making it inside."

The group moved with caution, their steps light and deliberate. They kept to the shadows, using the natural terrain to conceal their approach. Every now and then, a construct would pass by, its glowing eyes scanning the area, but the group managed to remain unseen.

As they neared the citadel's outer wall, Ethan spotted a narrow passage partially concealed by debris. "This way," he whispered, leading the group toward the hidden entrance. The passage was tight, forcing them to move single file, but it offered a way into the citadel without attracting the attention of the guardians.

The passage opened into a dimly lit corridor, the walls lined with ancient, rusting pipes and cables. The air was thick with the scent of oil and decay, and the faint sound of machinery echoed through the hall. The group paused, listening for any signs of movement.

"We're in," Astra whispered, her voice barely audible. "Now we need to find the artifact and get out before Serath's forces catch wind of us."

Kael nodded; his expression grim. "Let's move quickly. The longer we stay here, the greater the risk."

They pressed on, deeper into the heart of the citadel, knowing that the challenges ahead would test their skills and resolve like never before.

SCENE 2 - YEAR 3127 - DAY 052: LABYRINTH OF MACHINES

The corridor led them into the heart of the citadel—a vast, labyrinthine chamber filled with ancient, deadly machinery. The walls were lined with gears, cogs, and chains, all connected to massive engines that rumbled deep within the citadel's core. The floor was a network of conveyor belts and metal grates, and the air was thick with steam and the acrid smell of burning oil.

Ethan's eyes widened as he took in the sight before him. "This place… it's incredible. It's like a giant machine, every part working together to keep the citadel running. But it's also dangerous. One wrong move, and we could be crushed, sliced, or worse."

Zephyr let out a low whistle, his gaze sweeping over the labyrinth. "I'm glad we brought you along, Ethan. This is definitely your area of expertise."

Ethan nodded, already analyzing the machinery. "We need to move carefully. I can disable some of the traps, but we'll have to avoid most of the security systems.

They're too complex and ancient for me to fully override."

Astra watched Ethan work, her expression tense. "We're counting on you, Ethan. We need to get through this labyrinth and find the artifact."

The group followed Ethan's lead as he guided them through the labyrinth, his hands deftly manipulating wires and circuits to disable traps and unlock doors. They moved with precision, avoiding the deadly machinery that whirred and clanked all around them.

At one point, they reached a narrow walkway suspended over a massive pit filled with grinding gears and spinning blades. The walkway was barely wide enough for one person, and it swayed dangerously with every step.

Kael took the lead, his movements careful and deliberate. "Stay close and don't look down," he advised, his voice calm despite the perilous situation.

One by one, they crossed the walkway, their hearts pounding with each step. As they neared the other side, a section of the walkway gave way with a loud crash, sending debris tumbling into the pit below. Liora gasped, but Kael quickly grabbed her hand, steadying her.

"We're almost there," Kael reassured her, his grip firm.

Finally, they reached the other side, their breaths coming in ragged gasps. Ethan wiped the sweat from his brow, his face pale but determined. "We're close. I can feel it. The artifact is just ahead."

The group pressed on, navigating the last few twists and turns of the labyrinth. The sound of machinery grew louder, the air thickening with steam as they descended deeper into the citadel's core.

At last, they reached a massive set of doors, their surfaces engraved with intricate patterns and symbols. Ethan studied the door for a moment before nodding. "This is it. Beyond these doors lies the artifact."

Astra stepped forward, her hand resting on the door's cold surface. "Then let's finish this," she said, her voice filled with resolve.

With a deep breath, Ethan activated the door's mechanism, and the massive doors slowly creaked open, revealing the chamber beyond.

SCENE 3 - YEAR 3127 - DAY 053: CHAMBER OF ECHOES

The chamber beyond the doors was vast and eerily silent, the only sound being the faint echo of their footsteps on the cold stone floor. The walls were lined with shelves filled with ancient scrolls and books; their pages yellowed with age. At the center of the chamber stood a large, circular table, upon which lay an open tome, its pages glowing faintly with an otherworldly light.

Astra approached the table cautiously, her eyes scanning the room for any signs of danger. "This place... it's filled with knowledge. These are records from centuries ago, maybe even millennia."

Kael moved to one of the shelves, pulling out a scroll and unrolling it carefully. "These writings... they detail the history of Serath's rebellion. This citadel was once a place of great learning, a repository of knowledge. But now it's been corrupted."

Draven's eyes narrowed as he examined the room. "The knowledge here could be dangerous. If Serath's forces find this place..."

Liora nodded, her expression grave. "We need to take what we can and destroy the rest. We can't let this knowledge fall into the wrong hands."

Ethan approached the tome on the table, his eyes widening as he read the text. "This is it. This tome contains the knowledge we've been seeking. It details the location of the other artifacts, and it explains how they can be used to defeat Serath."

Astra's eyes lit up with determination. "Then we need to take it with us. This knowledge is too valuable to leave behind."

As she reached for the tome, the ground beneath them began to tremble, and the air filled with the sound of grinding gears. The citadel's defenses had been triggered, and they could hear the distant clanking of approaching constructs.

"Serath's forces are closing in," Zephyr warned, drawing his weapon. "We need to get out of here, now."

Astra grabbed the tome, and the group quickly made their way back toward the entrance. The chamber of echoes had revealed the secrets they sought, but it had also awakened the citadel's ancient guardians. They had no choice but to fight their way out.

SCENE 4 - YEAR 3127 - DAY 054: ARTIFACT OF KNOWLEDGE

The group sprinted through the citadel's corridors, the sound of pursuing constructs growing louder with each step. They could feel the vibrations of the citadel's ancient machinery as it reactivated, gears grinding and pistons firing in response to their intrusion.

Ethan led the way, his mind racing as he calculated the quickest route back to the entrance. "We're almost there! Just a little further!" he shouted over the din.

As they rounded a corner, they entered a large chamber with a high, vaulted ceiling. In the center of the room stood a pedestal, upon which rested the artifact they had been seeking—a tome of knowledge, its cover adorned with intricate symbols that seemed to pulse with energy.

Astra's eyes locked onto the artifact, her heart pounding with anticipation. "That's it! The Artifact of Knowledge!"

Before they could reach the pedestal, the walls of the chamber began to shift, and from hidden compartments emerged mechanical guardians—hulking constructs of metal and stone, their eyes glowing with a menacing red light.

"Defend the artifact!" Kael commanded, drawing his sword and charging toward the nearest construct. His blade clashed against the metal, sending sparks flying as he fought to keep the guardians at bay.

Liora moved to Astra's side, her hands glowing with healing energy. "I'll protect you while you retrieve the artifact!"

Draven darted through the shadows, his daggers flashing as he struck at the constructs with precision. "We need to take them down quickly! More are coming!"

Zephyr and Ethan worked together, using their combined knowledge of machinery and strategy to disable the constructs. Zephyr fired his energy blaster at the weak points Ethan identified, while Ethan manipulated the controls on his wrist device to disrupt the constructs' internal systems.

Astra focused her energy on the artifact, her staff glowing as she reached out to it. As her fingers brushed the tome's surface, a surge of knowledge flooded her mind, and she felt a deep connection to the ancient wisdom contained within.

But the moment she touched the artifact, the citadel's defenses activated in full force. The constructs began to multiply, and the chamber filled with the deafening roar of machinery as more guardians were summoned to protect the artifact.

"We need to get out of here!" Astra shouted, clutching the tome tightly to her chest.

Kael nodded; his expression grim as he fought off another construct. "We're with you! Let's move!"

With the artifact in hand, the group fought their way back toward the entrance, the citadel's defenses closing in around them. The walls shook with the force of the machinery, and the ground beneath them trembled as the constructs pursued them relentlessly.

But the group's determination and unity saw them through. They fought with everything they had, pushing back the tide of constructs as they made their escape.

As they burst through the citadel's main entrance, the cold air of the wasteland hit them like a shock. They had escaped the labyrinth of machines and retrieved the artifact, but their ordeal was far from over.

SCENE 5 - YEAR 3127 - DAY 055: SIEGE OF THE CITADEL

The group barely had time to catch their breath before they were besieged by Serath's forces. The citadel's guardians had alerted Serath's army, and now the wasteland surrounding the citadel was filled with shadowy figures, their eyes glowing with malevolent intent.

"Serath's forces are here! They've surrounded us!" Zephyr shouted, his eyes scanning the horizon for any sign of an escape route.

Kael gritted his teeth, his sword at the ready. "We'll have to fight our way out. There's no other option."

Astra looked to the artifact in her hands, its energy pulsing with a steady rhythm. "We can use the artifact to defend ourselves. It holds the knowledge we need to turn the tide."

The group formed a defensive circle, their weapons at the ready as Serath's forces closed in. The air was thick with tension, the sound of clashing metal and the cries of battle echoing through the wasteland.

Liora chanted a spell, creating a protective barrier around the group. "This will hold them off for a while, but it won't last forever. We need to find a way to break through their lines."

Ethan's mind raced as he analyzed the situation. "We can use the citadel's defenses against them. If we can lure them into the open, we can activate the remaining constructs to attack Serath's forces."

Zephyr nodded; his expression determined. "It's a risky plan, but it might be our only chance."

The group fought with all their might, using the knowledge contained within the artifact to outmaneuver and outsmart Serath's forces. They activated the citadel's remaining constructs, turning the ancient guardians against the invaders.

The battle raged on, the wasteland filled with the sounds of clashing metal and the roar of explosions. The group fought with everything they had, but the enemy's numbers seemed endless.

Just as it seemed they would be overwhelmed, Kael let out a battle cry, rallying his companions. "We can't give up now! We've come too far!"

With renewed determination, the group pushed forward, breaking through the enemy's lines and creating a path to safety.

As they made their escape, the citadel behind them began to collapse, the ancient structure crumbling under the strain of the battle. The ground shook, and the sky was filled with dust and debris as the citadel was reduced to ruins.

But the group had succeeded. They had retrieved the Artifact of Knowledge and escaped Serath's forces, though they were battered and bruised.

SCENE 6 - YEAR 3127 - DAY 056: REGROUPING AND REFLECTION

The group found a safe place to rest, a hidden alcove in the cliffs overlooking the wasteland. The air was cool and still, the chaos of the battle left far behind.

Astra sat with the artifact in her lap, her mind racing as she tried to process the knowledge it contained. "This artifact... it holds so much power. But it's also a heavy burden."

Kael tended to his wounds; his expression serious. "We've taken a great risk by retrieving it. Serath will stop at nothing to take it from us."

Liora knelt beside Astra, her healing light soothing the cuts and bruises they had sustained in the battle. "We've gained valuable knowledge, but we've also made ourselves a target. We need to be cautious moving forward."

Draven kept watch, his eyes scanning the horizon for any signs of danger. "We should keep moving. Serath's forces won't give up that easily."

Zephyr nodded; his expression thoughtful. "We need to regroup and plan our next move. The Abyss of the Forgotten is our next destination, but we can't afford to rush in unprepared."

Ethan adjusted his equipment, his mind already working on strategies for the challenges ahead. "The knowledge we've gained here will be crucial. We need to study it carefully and use it to our advantage."

As the group rested and reflected on their journey, they knew that the challenges ahead would be even greater. But they also knew that they were stronger together and that their unity would see them through.

"We've come this far," Astra said, her voice filled with determination. "We can't turn back now. The fate of our world depends on us."

With the Artifact of Knowledge in their possession and their resolve stronger than ever, the group prepared to continue their journey into the unknown. The Abyss of the Forgotten awaited them, and they knew that it would test them in ways they had never imagined.

But they were ready. They were united. And they would not be defeated.

CHAPTER 6:

ABYSS OF THE FORGOTTEN

SCENE 1 - YEAR 3127 - DAY 057: DESCENT INTO THE ABYSS

THE GROUP STOOD AT THE EDGE OF THE ABYSS OF THE FORGOTTEN, A GAPING CHASM THAT SEEMED TO STRETCH ENDLESSLY INTO THE DARKNESS BELOW. THE AIR AROUND THEM WAS THICK WITH A SENSE OF FOREBODING, AND THE FAINT WHISPERS OF LOST SOULS ECHOED UP FROM THE DEPTHS, CARRYING WITH THEM THE WEIGHT OF DESPAIR AND FORGOTTEN MEMORIES. THE VERY GROUND BENEATH THEIR FEET SEEMED TO TREMBLE WITH THE PRESENCE OF ANCIENT SORROWS, AND A CHILL RAN DOWN EACH OF THEIR SPINES AS THEY PEERED INTO THE VOID.

Astra tightened her grip on her staff, the light at its tip flickering as if struggling to maintain its glow against the oppressive darkness. "This is it," she said quietly, her voice barely audible over the haunting whispers. "The Abyss of the Forgotten."

Kael stepped forward, his hand resting on the hilt of his sword as he surveyed the descent. "The air here is thick with despair. We'll need to stay close and be vigilant. This place… it plays on your fears and doubts."

Draven's eyes narrowed as he scanned the path ahead. "It's more than just fear. The abyss has a way of drawing out the darkness within. We'll need to be prepared for whatever it throws at us."

Liora took a deep breath, her hands glowing with a soft, calming light. "The lost souls here are trapped, bound by Serath's influence. We must tread carefully, or we risk becoming lost ourselves."

Zephyr, ever the optimist, tried to lighten the mood. "Well, at least we know what we're up against. We've faced worse, haven't we?"

Ethan adjusted his equipment, his mind already working through possible strategies. "Let's focus on getting through this safely. We'll need to be methodical—one step at a time."

The group began their descent into the abyss, the path narrow and treacherous. The walls of the chasm seemed to close in around them, the darkness growing thicker with each step. The light from Astra's staff cast long, distorted shadows on the walls, creating an eerie, otherworldly atmosphere.

As they descended deeper, the whispers grew louder, the voices of the lost souls merging into a mournful chorus. The ground beneath their feet was uneven and slick, and more than once, one of them nearly slipped into the void.

The abyss seemed to have a will of its own, twisting the path and creating obstacles that tested their resolve. At times, the group had to jump across wide gaps, the darkness below threatening to swallow them whole. At other times, they had to climb over jagged rocks and navigate narrow ledges that crumbled beneath their weight.

But it wasn't just the physical challenges that they faced. As they descended, each member of the group began to feel the abyss's influence seeping into their minds, dredging up old fears and doubts. Kael's thoughts drifted to past battles where he had failed to protect those he cared about. Draven was haunted by memories of times when his cunning had led to unintended consequences. Liora felt the weight of every life she couldn't save, while Zephyr struggled with the fear of losing his adventurous spirit to the crushing despair around him. Ethan found himself questioning the limits of his knowledge and whether it would ever be enough to overcome the challenges ahead.

Astra, too, felt the darkness pressing in on her, the voices of the lost souls whispering doubts into her mind. But she shook her head, refusing to let the abyss take hold. "We must keep going," she urged, her voice steady. "We can't let this place break us."

With each step, the group drew closer together, their bond strengthening as they supported one another through the trials of the abyss. They knew that they would need to rely on each other more than ever if they were to emerge from the darkness.

SCENE 2 - YEAR 3127 - DAY 058:
RIVER OF SOULS

After what felt like an eternity of navigating the treacherous path, the group reached a cavernous chamber deep within the abyss. The air was thick and heavy, and a faint glow emanated from the far end of the chamber, where a dark, swirling river wound its way through the rock.

The group stood at the edge of the river, staring into the dark waters. The surface of the river seemed to ripple with the faces of lost souls, their expressions twisted with despair and longing. The river whispered to them, the voices of the souls beckoning them to step closer, to surrender to the darkness.

"We need to cross," Ethan said, his voice barely a whisper. "But the pull of the spirits… it's strong."

Astra nodded, her face pale. "The souls trapped here are bound by Serath's influence. They seek to pull us into the depths with them."

Liora stepped forward, her hands glowing with healing light. "I can calm the spirits, but it will take all of my strength. We must cross quickly before the river overwhelms us."

Kael tightened his grip on his sword, his gaze fixed on the river. "We'll stay close. Liora, we'll protect you while you work your magic."

Draven's eyes darted around the chamber, searching for any sign of danger. "We need to move quickly. The longer we stay here, the more vulnerable we are."

Zephyr gave Liora an encouraging nod. "We're with you, Liora. Let's get through this together."

Liora closed her eyes and began to chant, her voice soothing and melodic. The glow around her hands grew brighter, and the light spread outward, casting a warm, calming aura over the river. The faces of the lost souls began to soften, their expressions of despair replaced with a peaceful serenity.

As the light spread across the river, the water began to part, creating a narrow, shimmering path that led to the other side. The voices of the souls grew quieter, their pull weakening as Liora's magic took hold.

"Now," Liora urged, her voice strained with effort. "We need to move now."

The group hurried across the path, their steps quick and cautious. The river seemed to pulse with energy beneath them, and the faint whispers of the souls still reached out, but the light of Liora's magic kept them at bay.

As they reached the other side, the path behind them began to close, the water rushing back to fill the gap. Liora's light flickered and then faded as she collapsed to her knees, exhausted from the effort.

Kael was at her side in an instant, helping her to her feet. "You did it, Liora. We made it across."

Liora nodded weakly, her breathing heavy. "The spirits… they're at peace now. But we must keep moving. The abyss is not done with us yet."

Astra placed a hand on Liora's shoulder, offering her strength. "Thank you, Liora. Your light guided us through the darkness. We'll rest once we're out of this place."

With renewed determination, the group continued their journey, knowing that the challenges ahead would only grow more difficult. But they were one step closer to their goal, and they knew that as long as they stood together, they could overcome the darkness of the abyss.

SCENE 3 - YEAR 3127 - DAY 059: CHAMBER OF DESPAIR

The path through the abyss led them to another vast chamber, this one even darker and more foreboding than the last. The walls of the chamber were lined with twisted, gnarled roots that seemed to pulse with a life of their own, and the air was thick with the scent of decay and despair.

At the center of the chamber stood a series of stone platforms, each one surrounded by a swirling vortex of shadows. The air was heavy with the weight of unseen eyes, and the oppressive atmosphere pressed down on the group like a physical force.

"This place… it's filled with darkness," Astra murmured, her voice barely audible. "I can feel it pressing in on us."

Kael's expression was grim as he surveyed the chamber. "This is a place of despair, meant to break the spirit and shatter the will. We must stay strong and support each other."

Draven's eyes narrowed as he studied the platforms. "There's something about those shadows… They're not natural. They're meant to test us, to make us face our greatest fears."

Liora shivered, wrapping her arms around herself as the cold seeped into her bones. "This place… it wants to consume us. We must resist it, or we'll be lost."

Ethan adjusted his equipment, his face set with determination. "We've faced worse. We can get through this if we stay focused."

As they approached the platforms, the shadows began to swirl more violently, and the air grew colder. Each member of the group felt a sense of dread creeping over them, as if the very walls of the chamber were closing in.

Suddenly, the shadows lashed out, wrapping around each of them and pulling them toward the platforms. The world around them blurred, and they found themselves standing alone on separate platforms, surrounded by darkness.

Astra blinked, her heart pounding as she realized she was alone. The shadows whispered to her, taunting her with her deepest fears and doubts. She saw visions of her companions abandoning her, of the light within her fading, of the world falling into darkness because she wasn't strong enough to save it.

Kael stood on his own platform, his sword in hand, but the shadows around him were relentless. They whispered of battles lost, of comrades fallen because he wasn't strong enough. He saw himself failing again and again, unable to protect those he cared about.

Draven found himself surrounded by shadows that took the form of the enemies he had outwitted in the past. But this time, they were stronger, faster, and more cunning. No matter how hard he tried, he couldn't outmaneuver them, and they overwhelmed him with ease.

Liora faced shadows that took the form of the lives she couldn't save. The faces of those who had died despite her best efforts haunted her, their voices accusing her of failing them, of not being powerful enough to heal them.

Zephyr's platform was surrounded by shadows that took the form of the very adventures he had once relished. But now, they twisted into nightmares, with every step he took leading to ruin and loss. The thrill of discovery was replaced with the terror of the unknown.

Ethan stood on his platform, surrounded by shadows that took the form of machines he couldn't control, of knowledge slipping through his fingers. The shadows whispered that his inventions would never be enough, that he would always be one step behind, that his knowledge would fail him when he needed it most.

Each of them faced their own personal trial, the darkness preying on their deepest fears and insecurities. For a moment, it seemed as if the abyss would succeed in breaking them, in shattering their resolve.

But then, a soft light began to glow in the distance, cutting through the darkness. It was the light of Astra's staff, faint but unwavering. It pulsed with a steady rhythm, a beacon of hope in the darkness.

One by one, the group members reached out for the light, their hands grasping for the connection that would bring them back to each other. The light grew stronger with each connection, until it enveloped the entire chamber in a warm, golden glow.

The shadows recoiled, hissing and writhing as the light drove them back. The visions faded, and the group found themselves standing together once more, the platforms beneath them solid and the darkness retreating.

"We're stronger together," Astra said, her voice filled with resolve. "We won't let this place break us."

Kael nodded, his grip on his sword tightening. "We've faced our fears, and we've overcome them. We'll keep moving forward."

Liora's hands glowed with healing light as she reached out to comfort her companions. "The darkness can't touch us as long as we stand united."

Draven's eyes gleamed with determination. "We've outwitted the abyss. Now, let's finish this."

Zephyr's confident smile spread across his face. "This is just another challenge on our journey. We'll face it head-on, like we always do."

Ethan adjusted his equipment, his mind focused and clear. "We've got this. We'll keep moving forward, no matter what."

With the darkness defeated, the group continued their journey through the abyss, their spirits stronger than ever. They knew that the challenges ahead would be even greater, but they also knew that they were ready to face them together.

SCENE 4 - YEAR 3127 - DAY 060: LOST GUARDIAN

As they pressed deeper into the abyss, the group felt a change in the air. The oppressive darkness began to give way to a strange, pulsing energy that seemed to emanate from the very walls of the chasm. The path ahead grew narrower, the walls closing in around them as if guiding them toward something.

Finally, they emerged into a vast, open chamber, the air thick with a sense of ancient power. At the center of the chamber stood a massive figure, its form towering above them like a mountain. The figure was clad in ancient armor, its surface cracked and worn with age, and its eyes glowed with a sickly, green light.

Astra's eyes widened as she took in the sight of the guardian. "This… this is the guardian of the abyss. But it's been corrupted by Serath's influence."

Kael drew his sword, his expression grim. "We'll have to fight it. But how do we defeat something like this?"

Draven's eyes narrowed as he studied the guardian. "It's been corrupted, but it's still a guardian. If we can purify it, we might be able to turn it back to our side."

Liora nodded, her hands glowing with healing light. "I can try to cleanse the corruption, but I'll need time. We'll have to hold it off until then."

Zephyr readied his weapon, his expression determined. "We'll buy you as much time as you need, Liora. Let's do this."

Ethan adjusted his equipment, his mind racing as he analyzed the guardian. "There's a weak point in its armor, just above the chest plate. If we can strike there, we might be able to weaken it long enough for Liora to work her magic."

The group prepared for battle, their hearts pounding with a mix of fear and determination. The guardian let out a deafening roar, the sound reverberating through the chamber like a thunderclap. Its massive form began to move, each step shaking the ground beneath their feet.

Kael charged forward, his sword flashing as he struck at the guardian's legs, trying to slow its advance. The guardian's armor was tough, but Kael's blows were powerful, and the metal began to crack under the force of his attacks.

Draven darted around the guardian, his daggers flashing as he struck at its joints, seeking to disable its movements. His strikes were quick and precise, and the guardian's movements grew more sluggish with each hit.

Zephyr fired his energy blaster at the guardian's weak points, his shots finding their mark with deadly accuracy. The guardian roared in pain as the energy blasts seared through its armor, exposing the corrupted flesh beneath.

Ethan worked quickly, using his equipment to scan the guardian's energy patterns and identify the source of the corruption. "It's feeding off the energy of the abyss," he called out. "If we can cut off its connection, we can weaken it!"

Liora stood at the back of the group, her hands raised as she chanted a purification spell. The glow around her hands grew brighter and brighter, the light spreading out toward the guardian.

As the light touched the guardian, it recoiled, its movements growing more erratic as the corruption began to weaken. Liora's voice grew stronger as she poured all of her energy into the spell, her determination unwavering.

The guardian let out one final roar as the light of Liora's spell engulfed it, its form shaking violently as the corruption was driven out. The sickly green glow in its eyes faded, replaced by a soft, golden light.

The guardian's massive form began to shrink, its armor crumbling away to reveal a smaller, more human-like figure beneath. The light around it grew brighter, and the group watched in awe as the guardian was restored to its former self.

Astra stepped forward; her voice filled with reverence. "The guardian… it's been purified."

The guardian knelt before them; its head bowed in gratitude. "Thank you," it said, its voice deep and resonant. "I was lost to the darkness, but you have brought me back to the light."

Kael sheathed his sword, his expression one of respect. "We did what we had to do. The abyss is a dangerous place, but we're here to restore balance."

The guardian nodded, rising to its feet. "The abyss holds many secrets, and not all of them are dark. You have proven yourselves worthy, and I will grant you access to the next artifact."

SCENE 5 - YEAR 3127 - DAY 061: SHATTERED MEMORY

The guardian led the group to a hidden chamber deep within the abyss, its walls lined with ancient, glowing crystals. At the center of the chamber stood a pedestal, upon which rested a large, crystal shard. The shard pulsed with a soft, rhythmic light, and the air around it was filled with a sense of profound knowledge and ancient wisdom.

"The Shattered Memory," the guardian said, its voice filled with reverence. "This crystal holds the memories of the ancient civilization that once thrived here. It contains the knowledge you seek."

Astra stepped forward; her eyes locked on the crystal. "This is the artifact we've been searching for."

The guardian nodded; its expression solemn. "But be warned, the knowledge contained within the crystal is both a gift and a burden. It will show you the truth, but it may also reveal things you were not prepared to face."

Kael placed a hand on Astra's shoulder, offering her strength. "We're in this together, Astra. Whatever the crystal reveals, we'll face it as a team."

Liora's hands glowed with healing light as she reached out to touch the crystal. "The knowledge within this crystal… it can heal the wounds of the past and guide us toward the future."

Draven's eyes gleamed with determination. "We'll use this knowledge to defeat Serath and restore balance to the world."

Zephyr grinned; his adventurous spirit undiminished. "Another piece of the puzzle. Let's see what it has to offer."

Ethan adjusted his equipment, his mind already racing with the possibilities. "The knowledge in this crystal could be the key to understanding Serath's plans. We need to study it carefully."

Astra reached out and touched the crystal, and the moment her fingers made contact, a surge of energy flowed through her. Visions filled her mind—images of the ancient civilization that once thrived in the abyss, of their achievements and their downfall. She saw the rise of Serath and the corruption that spread through the land, turning the once-great civilization into a twisted, forsaken shadow of its former self.

The visions were overwhelming, but Astra held on, her grip on the crystal tightening as she absorbed the knowledge within. The memories of the ancient civilization flowed into her, their hopes and dreams, their triumphs and failures. She saw the truth of Serath's corruption, and the dark influence that had twisted the land and its people.

Finally, the visions began to fade, and Astra found herself standing once more in the chamber, the crystal shard in her hand. She took a deep breath, her heart heavy with the weight of the knowledge she had gained.

"The guardian was right," she said quietly. "The knowledge in this crystal… it's powerful, but it's also a burden. We know more about Serath's plans now, but we also know how much is at stake."

Kael nodded; his expression serious. "We'll use this knowledge to stop Serath. We have to."

Liora placed a comforting hand on Astra's arm. "We're stronger now, Astra. We have the knowledge we need to move forward."

Draven's voice was calm and steady. "We've come this far. We won't let Serath win."

Zephyr chuckled; his excitement evident. "We've got this. The adventure continues."

Ethan adjusted his equipment, his mind focused and clear. "We'll study the crystal carefully. It could be the key to defeating Serath."

The guardian watched them with a solemn expression. "You have passed the trials of the abyss, and you have gained the knowledge you seek. But your journey is not yet over. The abyss holds one final challenge before you can leave."

SCENE 6 - YEAR 3127 - DAY 062: CLIMBING BACK TO THE LIGHT

The group began their ascent from the abyss, the crystal shard now safely in their possession. The path ahead was steep and treacherous, the walls of the chasm closing in around them as they climbed toward the light above.

But the abyss was not done with them yet.

As they climbed, the shadows of the abyss began to stir, the darkness around them growing thicker and more oppressive. The whispers of the lost souls returned, louder and more insistent, pulling at their minds and threatening to drag them back into the depths.

Astra gritted her teeth, her grip on the crystal shard tightening. "We're almost there. We can't let the abyss pull us back."

Kael led the way, his sword at the ready as he cut through the shadows that reached for them. "Keep moving! We're not giving up now!"

Draven moved quickly, his daggers flashing as he struck at the shadows, his movements quick and precise. "We're stronger than this. The abyss won't take us."

Liora's hands glowed with healing light as she chanted a protective spell, the light forming a barrier around them as they climbed. "Stay close! The light will guide us!"

Zephyr and Ethan followed closely; their expressions determined as they fought off the shadows that tried to pull them back. "We're almost there!" Zephyr shouted; his voice filled with hope. "Just a little further!"

Ethan adjusted his equipment, his mind focused on the task ahead. "We'll make it. Just keep moving."

The climb was grueling, the shadows relentless in their attempts to drag them back into the abyss. But the group pressed on, their determination unwavering as they fought their way toward the light.

Finally, after what felt like an eternity, they emerged into the light above, the oppressive darkness of the abyss left far behind. The air was fresh and clean, the sky above clear and bright. The group collapsed onto the ground, their breaths coming in ragged gasps as they basked in the warmth of the sun.

"We made it," Astra said, her voice filled with relief. "We made it out of the abyss."

Kael nodded, his expression one of quiet satisfaction. "We faced the darkness and came out stronger. We're ready for whatever comes next."

Liora smiled, her eyes filled with warmth. "The light guided us through. We'll continue to follow it, no matter where it leads."

Draven's eyes gleamed with determination. "We've outwitted the abyss. Now, let's finish what we started."

Zephyr's grin was infectious. "The adventure continues. We're not done yet."

Ethan adjusted his equipment, his mind already working on the next challenge. "We have the knowledge we need. Now, let's use it to defeat Serath."

With the crystal shard in their possession and their spirits stronger than ever, the group prepared for the next leg of their journey. They knew that the challenges ahead would be even greater, but they were ready to face them together.

They had emerged from the abyss, and now, they were ready to bring the light back to the world.

CHAPTER 7:

ENCHANTED FOREST OF MIRRA

SCENE 1 - YEAR 3127 - DAY 063: ENTERING THE FOREST

THE GROUP STOOD AT THE EDGE OF THE ENCHANTED FOREST OF MIRRA, THE AIR AROUND THEM HUMMING WITH UNSEEN MAGICAL ENERGY. THE TOWERING TREES, THEIR BRANCHES WOVEN TOGETHER LIKE A LIVING CANOPY, FILTERED THE SUNLIGHT INTO A SOFT, ETHEREAL GLOW. THE FOREST ITSELF SEEMED ALIVE, FILLED WITH THE WHISPERS OF RUSTLING LEAVES AND DISTANT, UNEARTHLY BIRD CALLS. IT WAS A PLACE WHERE BEAUTY DANCED WITH DANGER, WHERE THE BOUNDARY BETWEEN REALITY AND ILLUSION DISSOLVED.

Astra stepped forward, her staff responding to the forest's magic with a soft glow. "This is the Enchanted Forest of Mirra," she murmured, her voice filled with wonder. "It's said to be a place of immense power, where the landscape shifts and magical creatures dwell."

Kael's grip tightened on his sword as he scanned their surroundings. "It may be beautiful, but we can't forget how dangerous it is. There are threats we won't see coming."

Draven studied the shadows between the trees with narrowed eyes. "This place is filled with illusions. We'll need more than our sight to guide us."

Liora stepped forward, her hands aglow with the soft light of healing. "The magic here is potent. If we're going to make it through, we must attune ourselves to it."

Zephyr's grin widened as he gazed into the forest. "It's like a living puzzle! Let's see what challenges it throws at us."

Ethan adjusted his equipment, his mind already churning through strategies. "We need to be cautious. This forest's magic could lead us astray if we aren't careful.

As the group entered the forest, the air grew cooler beneath the canopy, and the path ahead became winding and uncertain. It felt as though the forest was watching them, testing their resolve with every step. The trees shifted subtly; the undergrowth rearranged itself as if the very landscape was alive.

Astra's staff glowed brighter, her magic guiding them. "Stay close," she advised. "The magic here is strong. Don't let yourselves get separated."

The deeper they ventured, the more the landscape changed around them. The trees twisted into strange new shapes, and the ground seemed to shift beneath their feet. Beautiful creatures darted between the branches—shimmering butterflies whose wings sparkled like gemstones—but hidden in the shadows were beasts with glowing eyes, silently watching.

"The forest is watching us," Liora said softly, her connection to nature allowing her to sense its presence. "It's testing whether we're worthy."

Kael's expression was serious. "Then we'll prove that we are."

The further they walked, the more the forest shifted, leading them in circles, blocking their way. The pressure of the magic around them grew heavier with each step.

"We're close," Astra said with determination as her staff's glow intensified, cutting through the illusions. "We just need to keep going."

As they rounded a bend, the trees parted to reveal a large, open grove bathed in strange, shimmering light. The ground was covered in soft, mossy grass, and the air was filled with an unnatural sense of tranquility.

SCENE 2 - YEAR 3127 - DAY 064: ILLUSIONARY GROVE

The grove shimmered with otherworldly light, and the soft, moss-covered ground beckoned them to rest. The tall, ancient trees glowed faintly, as though filled with golden light. The place exuded peace, but there was something wrong—a sense that everything was too perfect.

As soon as they stepped into the grove, a wave of calm washed over them. The fears and worries that had gnawed at them since entering the forest began to fade, replaced by a feeling of contentment.

Astra frowned, her instincts alerting her to the deception. "Something's off. Be on your guard."

Kael's hand rested on the hilt of his sword. "It feels like a trap, but I can't sense anything tangible."

Draven's eyes narrowed as he scanned the grove. "It's an illusion. The forest is trying to lull us into a false sense of security."

Liora reached out with her healing light, attempting to feel the energy around them. "The magic here is potent, but it's not natural. It's trying to cloud our minds."

Zephyr's grin faded, realization dawning. "An illusion… but what is the forest hiding?"

Ethan adjusted his Quantum Linguist, his thoughts racing. "We need to find the real path. This grove is meant to distract us, to lead us astray."

They moved cautiously, but the more they tried to focus, the more difficult it became to distinguish reality from illusion. The light intensified, disorienting them, while the ground beneath their feet rippled like a mirage.

"We need to focus," Astra urged as her staff flared with light, but even her magic struggled against the grove's illusion.

Soon, each of them was lost in their own personal illusion. Kael found himself locked in a fierce battle, his sword clashing with unseen enemies. Liora wandered through a beautiful, endless garden, filled with vibrant flowers that whispered to her. Zephyr stood amid grand adventures, but they felt hollow, devoid of meaning. Ethan, surrounded by the hum of machines, tried in vain to escape a maze of mechanics.

Only Draven, a master of shadow magic, sensed the lie. Drawing on the shadows around him, he muttered to himself, "None of this is real." With the power of the shadows, he began to dispel the illusions.

The grove's light dimmed as Draven's magic unraveled the false images. The others began to wake from their illusions, the reality of the forest reasserting itself.

"Well done, Draven," Kael said, his voice full of gratitude. "You saved us."

"The forest won't stop here," Draven replied seriously. "We need to keep moving before it tries again."

With Draven's magic leading the way, the group found the hidden path and continued deeper into the forest. They had passed the first trial, their bond stronger than before.

SCENE 3 - YEAR 3127 - DAY 065: FAE COUNCIL

Deeper in the forest, the landscape shifted once again. The trees grew older, their trunks twisted with age, and the air was heavy with the scent of blooming flowers. Distant laughter echoed among the trees, creating an eerie yet beautiful atmosphere.

Eventually, they came upon a clearing filled with soft, golden light. In the center stood a circle of ancient stones, each inscribed with glowing runes. Within the circle, figures shimmered with otherworldly beauty—the Fae Council.

"These are the Fae of the forest," Astra whispered, her staff glowing faintly in recognition of their power.

Kael rested his hand on his sword hilt but did not draw it. "We need to be careful. The Fae are powerful, and they don't trust easily."

"They're watching us closely," Draven said. "We'll need to earn their trust."

Liora stepped forward. "If we show them we mean no harm, they might help us."

The lead Fae, a tall figure with silver hair and glowing eyes, stepped forward. "You are not of this forest. Why have you come to our domain?"

Astra spoke calmly. "We seek the artifact hidden within your forest, a tool of great power. We need it to restore balance to our world."

The Fae's gaze pierced through them. "This artifact is a relic of ancient guardians, capable of both creation and destruction. Why should we trust you?"

Kael stepped forward; his voice resolute. "We've faced many trials and proved our worth. We seek the artifact not for ourselves, but to protect the world from a great darkness."

The Fae regarded them for a moment before nodding slowly. "Your intentions seem pure. We will guide you, but the path ahead is fraught with trials."

SCENE 4 - YEAR 3127 - DAY 066: GUARDIAN BEAST

The path led the group deeper into the forest, the magic in the air growing heavier with every step. The trees closed in around them, the atmosphere thick with anticipation. It felt as if the forest itself was guiding them toward something monumental, a final test that would determine their worth.

At last, they entered a large clearing. The ground beneath them was soft with moss, and the air was filled with the fragrant scent of blooming flowers. But all eyes were drawn to the center of the clearing, where a massive creature stood, its form shimmering with raw power.

The Guardian Beast of the Enchanted Forest.

The creature was a blend of animal and magic, its body covered in iridescent scales that reflected light in a thousand shades. Its wings stretched wide, casting shadows over the clearing, and its claws dug deep into the earth. Its eyes, glowing with fierce intelligence, watched them intently, as if measuring their worth.

Astra stepped forward, her staff glowing in response to the beast's presence. "This is the final test. We must defeat the Guardian Beast to prove ourselves worthy of the artifact."

Kael drew his sword, the blade catching the light from the beast's shimmering scales. "We've faced powerful foes before. This will be no different. We fight together."

Draven moved silently to the side, his daggers flashing as he prepared to strike. "We'll need to outthink it as much as outfight it. This beast is no ordinary foe."

Liora's hands glowed with healing light, her focus on keeping the group strong during the fight. "Whatever happens, we stand united."

Zephyr's grin returned; his excitement palpable. "A battle against a magical beast? This is going to be epic."

Ethan adjusted his equipment, scanning the Guardian Beast's form with his translation device. His Quantum Linguist pinged, interpreting the energy patterns emitted by the creature. "It's drawing power from the forest. We'll need to disrupt its connection to weaken it."

With a thunderous roar, the Guardian Beast lunged toward them, its wings creating gusts of wind that shook the trees. Kael charged forward, meeting the beast head-on. His sword clashed with the creature's claws, sparks flying with every strike. The ground shook beneath the force of their battle.

Draven darted around the beast, his daggers flashing as he aimed for the creature's joints. But the beast's scales were nearly impenetrable, forcing him to use all his agility to stay out of its reach.

Liora stood at the center of the group, her healing light flowing to Kael and Draven, keeping them strong and steady. Her magic was the anchor that held the group together during the battle.

Zephyr's energy blaster hummed as he fired at the beast's wings, trying to cripple its ability to fly. His shots struck true, and the beast let out a roar of pain as its wings faltered.

Ethan's mind worked at lightning speed, his translation device scanning the beast's energy output. "Its connection to the forest is through its wings! If we take them down, it will lose its power."

Astra raised her staff high, channeling all her magic into a single, focused beam of light aimed at the beast's wings. The spell crackled with energy as it struck the creature, sending a wave of light through its body. The beast roared in agony, its wings crumbling under the force of Astra's magic.

With the beast weakened, Kael pressed his advantage, delivering a powerful blow to its legs, forcing the Guardian to its knees. Draven's daggers found their mark, slicing through the exposed joints, further disabling the creature's movement.

Liora's healing light continued to flow, keeping her companions strong as they fought. Zephyr's energy blasts rained down on the beast, blinding it and preventing it from retaliating.

Ethan, still focused on the beast's energy patterns, called out, "Now! It's vulnerable! Astra, finish it!"

With all her strength, Astra channeled one final spell, a blast of pure, radiant light that struck the Guardian Beast directly in the chest. The beast let out one last, mournful roar before collapsing to the ground, its wings crumpled and its body shimmering with fading energy.

As the dust settled, the group stood victorious, their breaths coming in ragged gasps. The Guardian Beast lay still, its eyes glowing faintly with peace rather than malice.

"You have proven yourselves," the Guardian Beast rumbled, its voice filled with a deep, resonant power. "The artifact you seek is within the heart of the forest. Go now, and take it with my blessing."

With those final words, the beast's body began to dissolve into shimmering light, its spirit returning to the forest. The ground where it had fallen glowed with a radiant sigil, pointing the way forward.

The group stood in awe, the weight of their victory sinking in. They had passed the final trial of the Enchanted Forest, and now the path to the artifact lay open before them.

SCENE 5 - YEAR 3127 - DAY 067: HEART OF THE FOREST

The glowing sigil left by the Guardian Beast guided the group through a narrow path deeper into the forest. The atmosphere around them changed, becoming more peaceful and reverent, as though the forest itself acknowledged their victory.

Soon, they arrived at the heart of the forest, a large, circular clearing surrounded by ancient, towering trees. At the center of the clearing stood an ancient tree, its bark intricately carved with runes and symbols that pulsed with a soft, green light. The tree's branches stretched high into the sky, and its roots seemed to connect with the very life force of the forest.

"This is it," Astra whispered as she approached the tree. Her staff glowed in response to the ancient magic that flowed through the heart of the forest. "The artifact is here, hidden within the tree."

The group gathered around the tree, studying the carvings that adorned its bark. The symbols told stories of ancient battles, guardians, and the flow of magic through the natural world. At the base of the tree was a small opening, just large enough for someone to reach inside.

Kael knelt beside the opening, his hand resting on the tree's bark. "There's something here, but it's protected by a riddle."

Draven's eyes narrowed as he examined the carvings. "The tree is testing our wisdom. We'll need to think carefully before we act."

Liora's hands glowed softly as she touched the tree's bark, sensing its life force. "The magic here is strong. We must approach with respect."

Zephyr's grin returned, though more subdued. "Another puzzle! Let's see what this tree has in store for us."

Ethan adjusted his equipment, his mind already working through possible answers. "We need to solve the riddle to unlock the artifact. Let's think it through."

As they studied the tree, a voice seemed to whisper from deep within, the words forming in their minds like a distant echo:

"I am the source of life and the keeper of secrets. I grow with the sun and the rain, and I wither in the darkness. I am both old and new, and I hold the wisdom of ages. What am I?"

The group fell silent, each of them contemplating the meaning of the riddle. The answer lay within the words, connected to the very essence of the tree and the magic that flowed through it.

Astra closed her eyes, reaching out with her magic. "The answer is life," she whispered. "The tree is the source of life, and it holds the wisdom of the ages."

Kael nodded, his hand resting on the tree. "Life grows with the sun and the rain, and it withers in the darkness. The tree is both ancient and new, a connection to the past and future."

Draven's eyes gleamed with understanding. "The tree is the key. We need to connect with its life force to unlock the artifact."

Liora's healing light intensified as she placed her hands on the tree's roots. "The tree's magic is strong. If we work together, we can unlock its secrets."

The group joined hands, channeling their energy into the tree. The ancient carvings glowed brighter, and the opening at the base of the tree widened, revealing the artifact hidden within.

Astra reached inside, her fingers trembling slightly as they brushed against the artifact. A surge of energy rushed through her, and she felt an immediate connection to the life force of the forest.

She pulled out the Staff of Life, a beautiful staff covered in intricate carvings that pulsed with a soft, green light. As she held it, she could feel its power strengthening her magic and enhancing her connection to the world around her.

Liora's eyes widened as she sensed the magic flowing through the staff. "This staff... it's connected to the forest's life force. It will enhance our abilities and deepen our bond."

Kael's voice was solemn. "We've gained a powerful tool, but we must use it wisely. The forest has entrusted us with its power."

Draven nodded. "We've passed the final test. Now, we continue our journey."

Zephyr's grin returned, full of excitement. "Another artifact in the bag! We're one step closer."

Ethan studied the staff, his mind already working on how to incorporate its power into their strategy. "The staff will be invaluable in the challenges ahead. We'll need to study its magic carefully."

With the Staff of Life in their possession, the group turned to leave the heart of the forest. They had passed the trials of the Enchanted Forest, and now, they were stronger and more united than ever.

SCENE 6 - YEAR 3127 - DAY 068:
A GIFT FROM THE FAE

As they made their way back toward the forest's edge, the group was once again met by the Fae Council. The Fae stood silently, their expressions a mixture of curiosity and respect. The air around them was thick with magic, and the forest seemed to hum with approval.

"You have passed the trials of the forest," the lead Fae said, their voice carrying a melodic echo. "You have proven yourselves worthy of the artifact, and the forest has accepted you."

Astra bowed her head. "We are honored. Thank you for trusting us with this power. We will use it wisely."

The lead Fae nodded, their silver hair catching the light. "The forest has granted you its power, and now, we will give you a gift to aid you on your journey."

The Fae raised their hands, and a soft, golden light enveloped the group. The light was warm and filled them with a sense of strength and peace. As the glow faded, each of them felt a surge of energy coursing through their bodies, their abilities enhanced by the forest's magic.

Kael felt his strength renewed, his sword now glowing faintly with golden light. Draven's connection to the shadows deepened, the darkness itself seeming to bend to his will. Liora's healing light burned brighter, filled with newfound power. Zephyr's energy blaster hummed with fresh energy, and Ethan's equipment buzzed with enhanced capabilities.

"The forest has given you its blessing," the lead Fae said. "You are now bound to the magic of Mirra. But remember, with great power comes great responsibility. Use it wisely."

Astra nodded; her expression resolute. "We will honor the trust the forest has placed in us. Thank you, honored Fae."

The Fae Council watched as the group prepared to leave, their eyes filled with both pride and sadness. "Go now, and may the light of the forest guide you."

With the Staff of Life and the Fae's blessing, the group left the Enchanted Forest of Mirra. Their hearts were filled with renewed strength, and they were ready to face the challenges that awaited them in the next leg of their journey.

CHAPTER 8:

DESERT OF FORGOTTEN DREAMS

SCENE 1 - YEAR 3127 - DAY 069: SCORCHING SANDS

AT THE EDGE OF THE DESERT OF FORGOTTEN DREAMS, THE GROUP STOOD, GAZING OUT AT THE VAST EXPANSE OF SHIMMERING SAND STRETCHING OUT AS FAR AS THE EYE COULD SEE. THE HEAT WAS SUFFOCATING, WITH THE BLAZING SUN HIGH IN A CLOUDLESS SKY REFLECTING OFF THE DUNES AND DISTORTING THE HORIZON. EVERY BREATH FELT HEAVY, FILLED WITH THE DRY SCENT OF SCORCHED EARTH AND THE FAINT WHISPERS OF A HOT WIND, CARRYING THE MEMORIES OF AN ANCIENT, FORGOTTEN PAST.

Astra shaded her eyes from the blinding light. Her staff glowed faintly as she attuned herself to the oppressive magic that seemed to permeate the desert. "This place," she murmured, her voice filled with awe and trepidation, "is the Desert of Forgotten Dreams. It's said that this heat can melt even the strongest resolve, turning dreams into dust."

Kael adjusted the straps of his gear, his muscles already straining under the intense heat. "We'll need to conserve energy," he said, scanning the horizon. "This desert is merciless. We need to reach the oasis before it breaks us."

Draven's sharp eyes swept over the dunes. "The desert is deceptive. Every shadow, every shimmer—it could be a trap. We must be vigilant if we want to make it through."

Liora, always mindful of the group's well-being, cast a cooling spell, her hands glowing with soft, green light. "This will help a little, but we'll have to work together to withstand this heat."

Zephyr's usual grin was undimmed, even under the blazing sun. "A challenge, sure. But nothing we can't handle! Let's find that oasis and cool off."

Ethan, already analyzing the environment with his equipment, adjusted his Universal Translator. His device, made from unique components sourced from his home world, began to hum softly, processing the data from the desert's magical interference. "We'll need to stay hydrated and keep a close eye on our path. This desert can turn against us at any moment."

With that, they began their trek into the desert. The sand shifted under their feet with every step, making the journey feel like an uphill battle. The sun's rays beat down with unrelenting intensity, each moment sapping their strength, the dry air burning their lungs. It was a test of both physical and mental endurance.

Astra's staff glowed brighter, a protective shield of light emanating from it to stave off the worst of the desert's heat. "The oasis is our only chance," she said, her voice tight. "We have to find it soon."

Kael wiped sweat from his brow and nodded. "Keep moving. Stopping here will only make things worse."

Draven, ever alert, squinted into the distance, his instincts telling him that not everything was as it seemed. "This desert has illusions layered into it. We can't trust what we see."

Liora's cooling spell kept them from overheating, but the relentless sun still weighed on their spirits. "We're getting closer," she assured them. "We just have to endure a little longer."

Zephyr's grin had faded, replaced with steely determination. "We've come too far to let a little heat stop us."

Ethan kept his device trained on the horizon, searching for signs of life or shelter. "We have to stay focused. The desert's magic could easily lead us astray."

Together, they pressed on, driven by sheer willpower and the knowledge that they could not afford to fail. The desert was testing them, and they would prove themselves stronger than its scorching heat.

SCENE 2 - YEAR 3127 - DAY 070: MIRAGE OF TEMPTATION

As the sun climbed higher, its heat grew more oppressive, distorting the air around them. The dunes seemed to stretch on forever, and their exhaustion grew with every step. The only sound was the shifting of sand beneath their feet and the occasional whisper of the wind.

Then, strange images began to appear in the distance—shimmering oases and lush greenery, impossible mirages flickering at the edges of their vision. At first, the group dismissed them, recognizing the tricks of the desert, but as they continued forward, the visions became more vivid and almost tangible.

Astra's staff glowed brighter as she sensed the strange shift in the desert's magic. "These aren't normal mirages," she warned, her voice tinged with caution. "They're too real… too dangerous."

Kael's hand rested instinctively on the hilt of his sword. "The desert is playing with our minds. We can't afford to fall for these tricks."

Draven's gaze darkened as he studied the illusions more closely. "These mirages aren't just illusions—they're traps, designed to draw us in and wear us down."

Liora extended her hands, her magic reaching out to feel the pulse of the desert. "The magic here is testing our will. If we give in, we'll lose our way."

Zephyr, his grin cautious now, chuckled grimly. "No way I'm falling for some fancy trick. We've got a real oasis to find."

Ethan adjusted his equipment, his Universal Translator working overtime to interpret the distortions in the desert's magical signature. "This desert isn't just testing us physically—it's trying to break us mentally. These mirages could disorient us if we aren't careful."

The group pressed on, but as they did, the mirages grew stronger, more tempting. Soon, each member of the group began to see visions of their deepest desires, their most cherished dreams playing out in the shifting sand.

Astra saw herself with her family, safe and happy in a beautiful garden. Kael envisioned his greatest victory, his enemies vanquished and his comrades cheering. Draven glimpsed a life free from the shadows that constantly pursued him. Liora saw herself surrounded by those she had healed, their gratitude warming her heart. Zephyr envisioned wild adventures, discovering hidden treasures in far-off worlds. Ethan saw himself solving the mysteries of the universe, surrounded by the greatest minds in history.

The allure was almost irresistible, but each of them knew the truth—the desert was trying to break them.

Astra's staff pulsed with light as she shook off the temptation. "These dreams are false. We can't give in."

Kael tightened his grip on his sword, his resolve hardening. "We won't be led astray by illusions."

Draven called upon the shadows, his magic cutting through the mirages. "I see through this deceit. The desert won't claim us."

Liora focused on the path ahead, her healing light guiding the way. "We won't lose our way here. We know our true purpose."

Zephyr's adventurous spirit refused to be dimmed by the desert's tricks. "Nice try, desert! But we're not falling for it."

Ethan tapped into his equipment, his Universal Translator identifying the energy patterns behind the illusions. "We'll stay on course. The desert won't defeat us."

With their determination strengthened, the group pushed forward, leaving the mirages behind. The desert had tried to break them with temptation, but they would not be swayed from their mission.

SCENE 3 - YEAR 3127 - DAY 071: SANDSTORM

As the sun began to set, casting long shadows over the dunes, a strange stillness settled over the desert. The heat had not abated, but there was a shift in the air—a sense of impending danger that put everyone on edge.

Zephyr's sharp instincts kicked in first. He felt the wind change, and his eyes narrowed as he scanned the horizon. "A storm's coming. A big one."

Kael glanced around, his hand tightening on his sword. "We need shelter. Fast. A sandstorm out here could bury us alive."

Draven's keen eyes darted over the dunes, searching for any sign of refuge. "There's no cover nearby. We'll have to face this storm head-on."

Liora's hands glowed with healing light, ready to shield the group from harm. "We need to stick together. This storm is going to test us."

Ethan adjusted his equipment, calculating their chances. "We'll need to use every tool we have. This storm could be deadly."

The first gust of wind hit them like a warning, a rush of hot air kicking up the sand. The sky darkened quickly, and the sound of the approaching storm grew louder— a low, ominous roar that echoed across the desert.

When the sandstorm hit, it was like being swallowed by a hurricane of sand and wind. Visibility vanished as the swirling sand engulfed them, and the roar of the storm drowned out everything.

Zephyr, sensing that this was his moment, stretched out his hands, summoning the power of the winds. His Universal Translator, designed to sync with the natural elements of his home world, crackled with energy as he manipulated the storm. "Stay close!" he shouted; his voice barely audible over the howling winds. "I can shield us, but we need to move quickly!"

The group huddled together as Zephyr formed a protective bubble of calm air around them, guiding the worst of the storm away from their path. Kael braced himself, keeping the group steady, while Draven, light on his feet, moved ahead to scout for shelter.

Finally, through the swirling sands, they spotted the faint outline of an ancient ruin, partially buried in the dunes. It was their only chance.

"There!" Ethan shouted, pointing toward the ruin. "That's our shelter!"

With Zephyr's wind control shielding them, the group made a dash toward the ruin. The storm raged around them, but they pressed on, driven by the need to survive.

They reached the ruins just as the storm reached its peak, the winds howling furiously outside as they took refuge within the stone walls. The ancient carvings on the walls seemed to glow faintly in the light of Astra's staff.

"We made it," Kael said, relief washing over him. "But we're not safe yet."

Draven ran his fingers over the carvings, deciphering the ancient symbols. "These markings—they're a map. They might lead us to the artifact."

Liora's healing light soothed the group's exhaustion. "We'll rest for now, but we can't stay here forever."

Zephyr, winded from controlling the storm, grinned through his exhaustion. "We've survived worse. We'll figure this out."

Ethan adjusted his Universal Translator, scanning the ancient writings for clues. "This ruin may hold the key to finding the oasis. Let's figure it out."

As the storm howled outside, the group gathered around the carvings, their minds focused on the next step of their journey. The desert had tested them, but they had survived. Now, they would use the knowledge of the past to find the oasis and retrieve the next artifact.

SCENE 4 - YEAR 3127 - DAY 072: ETERNAL MIRAGE

The storm outside eventually subsided, but the desert's magical interference remained, swirling ominously in the air. The group, still inside the ruins, felt the atmosphere grow thick with tension. The carvings on the walls, though ancient and weathered, seemed to pulse with life under the soft glow of Astra's staff.

Suddenly, the air shimmered, and the walls of the ruin seemed to warp, stretching and bending until reality itself felt unstable. Astra's staff flickered as she tightened her grip, her eyes narrowing.

"Something's wrong," she whispered, her voice tense. "This isn't just another storm. The desert is trying to trap us in an illusion."

Kael, his sword at the ready, scanned their surroundings. "It's like the mirages we saw earlier, but this time, it feels... stronger. Like it's trying to pull us in."

Draven's dark eyes narrowed as he drew on his shadow magic, sensing the trap. "This is no ordinary illusion. It's an enchantment—designed to keep us lost in this ruin forever."

Liora stretched out her hands, her healing light flickering as she attempted to dispel the illusion. "It's like a loop—meant to confuse us, make us forget why we're here."

Zephyr's grin faded into determination as the walls of the ruin continued to shift and blur. "We've got to break through it. We can't let the desert win."

Ethan adjusted his Universal Translator, which began to emit a soft pulse. His device was synced to the group's unique energy signatures, using their collective strength to push back against the enchantment. "We need to disrupt the magic around us. The key might be in the carvings."

As the group focused on deciphering the carvings, the illusion intensified, pulling at their minds and emotions. It was more than a mere mirage—this was the Eternal Mirage, a powerful enchantment designed to trap travelers in an endless loop of despair.

Astra's eyes widened as she felt the illusion tighten around her, showing her visions of her companions, lost and defeated, their bodies buried under the desert's sands. Kael gripped his sword tighter as he saw himself failing in battle, his comrades falling at his side. Draven felt the familiar weight of the shadows trying to consume him again, while Liora saw the faces of those she couldn't save, their eyes full of blame.

Zephyr struggled against the vision of endless wandering; his adventurous spirit dimmed by the monotony of the desert. Even Ethan, usually calm and collected, felt the pressure of his mind buckling under the weight of the illusion, his inventions failing and his calculations collapsing into chaos.

But the group knew better. They knew these were illusions—designed to prey on their insecurities and deepest fears.

Draven, focusing on the shadows, was the first to break free. His shadow magic flared, slicing through the layers of the illusion. "This isn't real," he muttered, his voice a beacon in the darkness. "None of this is real."

Astra's staff glowed brighter as she pushed back against the mirage with the light within her. "The Eternal One guides us," she said firmly, her voice steady. "We cannot fall here."

Kael slammed his sword into the ground, using its weight to ground himself in reality. "We've faced worse," he said through gritted teeth. "This desert won't defeat us."

Liora's healing magic burned brightly as she refocused, her hands glowing with renewed energy. "We will heal the wounds of the past and move forward."

Zephyr shook off the illusion with a grin. "Nice try, desert. We've got a mission to finish."

Ethan, his Universal Translator humming with the combined energy of the group, used the device to pinpoint the core of the illusion. "I've got it!" he shouted. "There—if we focus on that point, we can break through!"

Together, they channeled their energy, concentrating on the weak point in the illusion. The air shimmered one last time before reality snapped back into place. The ruins solidified around them, and the oppressive weight of the Eternal Mirage lifted.

"We did it," Astra said, relief flooding her voice. "We broke free."

But the group knew the desert's challenges weren't over yet.

SCENE 5 - YEAR 3127 - DAY 073:
OASIS OF MEMORY

After what seemed like an eternity of wandering through the oppressive sands, the group finally spotted something on the horizon—a faint shimmer of light. It was different from the mirages they had seen before. As they drew closer, the shimmering light solidified into a vibrant oasis surrounded by lush greenery and tall palms. The air cooled, and the scent of fresh water and blooming flowers washed over them like a balm.

Astra's staff glowed softly as they approached. "This is it," she whispered. "The Oasis of Memory."

The oasis was a place of tranquility, but they knew it wasn't merely a place to rest. It held the key to their next trial.

Kael wiped the sweat from his brow and gazed at the cool waters. "This feels… different. There's magic here."

Draven, ever cautious, studied the waters with narrowed eyes. "It's not just an oasis. The water holds memories both good and bad. We'll have to face the past to move forward."

Liora knelt at the water's edge, dipping her fingers into the cool water. Her eyes widened as she felt the magic flow through her. "The water is alive with memories of those who came before us. We must unlock its secrets."

Zephyr, always up for a challenge, cracked a grin. "We've come this far. Let's see what the oasis has in store."

Ethan, adjusting his Universal Translator, studied the magical signature of the water. "The water will show us the past memories of this place, of the ancient civilization that lived here. It's the only way to find the artifact."

The group knelt by the water's edge, watching as its surface shimmered with a soft, golden light. The light spread across the surface of the oasis, forming intricate patterns that seemed to dance before their eyes.

A voice echoed in their minds, soft and melodic. "To unlock the secrets of the past, you must first remember who you are. Drink from the waters of memory, and the truth shall be revealed."

Astra hesitated, then reached out, dipping her hand into the water. "We must drink," she said quietly. "The memories will guide us."

One by one, the group drank from the oasis, and as they did, visions filled their minds. They saw a thriving civilization, living in harmony with the magic of the desert. They saw the rise of Serath, his darkness spreading across the land, corrupting the people and turning the desert into a barren wasteland. They saw the creation of the artifact—a chalice of water, meant to preserve the memories of the ancient people and protect the future.

The visions were intense, overwhelming in their clarity. But the group held firm, knowing that these memories held the key to their mission.

As the visions faded, the waters of the oasis stilled, and in the center of the pool, an island appeared small, but lush with greenery. At the center of the island stood a pedestal, and resting upon it was a chalice, shimmering with golden light.

Astra rose, her heart pounding as she stepped toward the island. "The Chalice of Memory," she whispered. "This is the artifact we seek."

Kael followed; his expression determined. "We've unlocked the past. Now we must use it to defeat Serath."

Draven's shadow magic flickered as he prepared to retrieve the chalice. "The chalice will protect our minds from Serath's illusions."

Liora's hands glowed softly as she touched the chalice, her connection to the water deepening. "The memories will guide us. We must honor them."

Zephyr's grin returned, full of confidence. "Another win for us! We're one step closer to stopping Serath."

Ethan, his mind already planning ahead, nodded. "The chalice will be our defense against Serath's magic. We'll need it for the battles ahead."

With the Chalice of Memory in hand, the group left the oasis, ready for the final challenge that awaited them in the desert.

SCENE 6 - YEAR 3127 - DAY 074: DESERT'S EMBRACE

As they prepared to leave the oasis, the desert shifted again. The peaceful atmosphere was quickly replaced by a looming sense of danger, and from the horizon, a dark cloud began to rise. It wasn't another sandstorm—this was something far worse.

Serath's forces had found them.

Astra's staff glowed brighter as she prepared for battle. "Serath's forces… they've come for the chalice."

Kael drew his sword, his face hardening with resolve. "We've faced his soldiers before. We'll fight them off."

Draven, his shadow magic flaring, nodded. "The chalice will shield us from their illusions."

Liora's healing light pulsed, ready to protect the group. "We're stronger than we were before. We can do this."

Zephyr cracked his knuckles, his adventurous grin full of determination. "Bring it on. We're ready."

Ethan adjusted his Universal Translator, syncing it with the chalice's energy. "We'll use the chalice to protect our minds. Let's finish this."

The battle was intense, the air filled with the clash of steel and the crackle of magic. Serath's forces surged toward them, their numbers overwhelming, but the group held strong. Astra raised the chalice, its golden light creating a barrier around them, shielding their minds from the enemy's illusions.

Kael led the charge, cutting through enemy ranks with precision. Draven's shadows struck from every direction, confusing and disorienting the soldiers. Liora's healing magic kept them all on their feet, while Zephyr's energy blasts took down foes with pinpoint accuracy.

Ethan, calculating the enemy's movements, directed the group with precision. "Focus on their weaknesses! We've got this!"

The tide of battle slowly turned in their favor, and with a final blast of light from Astra's staff, Serath's forces were driven back into the desert.

As the dust settled, the group stood victorious, their hearts pounding with adrenaline and relief.

"We did it," Astra said, lowering the chalice. "We've won."

Kael sheathed his sword, nodding. "The desert's challenges are behind us. But we have more to face."

Draven's shadow magic flickered as he prepared for the next journey. "Serath won't stop, but neither will we."

Liora's healing light pulsed softly. "We've grown stronger. We're ready for what's next."

Zephyr grinned wide. "One step closer to victory!"

Ethan adjusted his equipment. "The chalice will guide us forward. Let's keep moving."

With the Chalice of Memory in hand and Serath's forces defeated, the group set off once more, ready for the trials that awaited them.

Together, they would face the darkness, armed with the power of the past and the strength of their bond.

CHAPTER 9:

ICE CAVES OF GLACIA

SCENE 1 - YEAR 3127 - DAY 075: FROZEN ENTRANCE

THE BITING COLD GREETED THE GROUP AS THEY STOOD AT THE ENTRANCE TO THE ICE CAVES OF GLACIA, THEIR BREATHS FORMING MISTY CLOUDS IN THE FRIGID AIR. THE VAST EXPANSE OF SNOW AND ICE STRETCHED BEFORE THEM, THE FROZEN GROUND CRUNCHING BENEATH THEIR BOOTS AS THEY APPROACHED THE MASSIVE GLACIER ARCHWAY LEADING INTO THE CAVES. EVEN WITH THEIR PROTECTIVE GEAR, THE COLD GNAWED AT THEIR BONES, DRAINING THEIR STRENGTH.

Guarding the entrance were two massive frost giants, encased in armor made of shimmering ice. Their icy breath created plumes of steam in the air as they stood vigilant, their eyes scanning for intruders.

Astra raised her staff, its soft glow illuminating the frozen landscape. She could feel the ancient magic embedded in the glacier. "These caves hold great power," she murmured, "but they are fraught with danger."

Kael tightened his grip on his sword, his muscles coiling in preparation. "We can't fight them head-on. We need another way in."

Draven's eyes narrowed as his shadow magic wrapped around them, concealing their movements. "The frost giants may be powerful, but they are slow. We might be able to sneak by them if we time it just right."

Liora's hands glowed softly as she cast a warmth spell, sending waves of heat through the group to stave off the cold. "The deeper we go, the colder it will get. We have to move quickly."

Zephyr's grin flickered, but he was still eager. "Just another challenge. We've outsmarted worse than this."

Ethan adjusted his Universal Translator, syncing it to their environment as he calculated potential strategies. "We'll have to use the element of surprise. If we move together, we can slip by unnoticed."

With Draven's shadow magic cloaking them, the group silently crept toward the entrance. The frost giants remained unaware, their massive forms standing like frozen sentinels. The harsh wind howled through the towering glaciers, but the group pressed on, their focus unshaken.

Astra's staff glowed brighter, casting a soft light to guide their way as they slipped past the towering guardians and toward the dark, gaping entrance of the cave.

"We made it," Zephyr whispered, his grin returning as they reached the threshold. "Now, let's see what these ice caves are hiding."

The air inside was colder, and as they took their first steps into the Ice Caves of Glacia, a sense of foreboding settled over them. Whatever awaited them in the icy depths, they were ready.

SCENE 2 - YEAR 3127 - DAY 076: CRYSTAL LABYRINTH

Once inside, the Ice Caves of Glacia revealed their stunning beauty. The walls were lined with crystalline structures that refracted the light from Astra's staff, casting dazzling patterns of color across the ice. The sound of dripping water echoed faintly through the cavern as the ice melted and refroze in an endless cycle.

But as breathtaking as the cave was, it was equally dangerous. The crystals created a labyrinth of mirrors, and the reflections twisted the paths in confusing directions, making it nearly impossible to tell which way was forward.

Astra's staff flickered brighter, trying to cut through the disorienting reflections. "The light is playing tricks on us," she said, her voice resonating with caution. "We'll need to find the true path."

Kael's hand remained on the hilt of his sword as he scanned the shimmering walls. "We need to be careful. These crystals might look beautiful, but they could easily mislead us."

Draven's shadow magic pulsated around him, ready to dispel the illusions. "The crystals are creating an intricate maze. We'll need more than just our eyes to navigate through."

Liora's healing magic flickered as she touched the crystalline walls, feeling the faint pulse of ancient magic within them. "The crystals are alive with old magic," she said quietly. "We need to respect their power."

Zephyr let out an appreciative whistle as he studied the intricate patterns. "A labyrinth of light and mirrors? Sounds like the perfect puzzle. Let's find the way out."

Ethan's Universal Translator hummed softly as he began analyzing the reflections. "We need to study the light's behavior. The path will be hidden in the distortions—if we focus, we can outmaneuver the illusions."

Together, the group ventured into the maze, each step careful and deliberate. Astra's staff guided them, its light cutting through the swirling patterns. Draven's shadow magic helped reveal false paths, and Ethan's calculations ensured they avoided the most deceptive parts of the labyrinth.

As they ventured deeper, the maze grew more complex, the temperature plummeting with every step. The crystals shifted and shimmered, creating illusions that seemed to trap them in an endless loop.

But Astra's focus never wavered. "We need to find the light's source," she reminded the group. "It will lead us through."

Finally, after what felt like hours of navigating the crystalline maze, they found a narrow passage hidden behind a particularly reflective wall. The crystals parted before them, revealing the way forward.

They had made it through the labyrinth, but they knew that their journey through the Ice Caves was far from over.

SCENE 3 - YEAR 3127 - DAY 077:
FROZEN HEART

The passage opened into a massive chamber, and the air turned so cold it felt like it could freeze their breath in their lungs. Icicles hung like deadly spears from the ceiling, and the walls were thick with layers of frost.

At the center of the room stood a massive, glowing crystal—pulsing with energy—the Frozen Heart. Its cold blue light bathed the chamber in an eerie glow, and the power emanating from it made the temperature drop even further.

"This is it," Astra said quietly, her breath visible in the frigid air. "The source of the cold. The Frozen Heart."

Kael unsheathed his sword, his eyes fixed on the glowing crystal. "We'll need to destroy it if we want to retrieve the artifact."

Draven's shadow magic flickered around him, a sharp contrast to the cold light of the heart. "The Frozen Heart controls the cold, but our warmth can fight back."

Liora raised her hands, the glow of her healing light struggling against the oppressive cold. "This will be our hardest battle yet."

Zephyr's grin was gone, replaced by a look of steely resolve. "We've got this. We've faced worse, and we'll win again."

Ethan adjusted his equipment, syncing the Universal Translator with the heart's energy signature. "The core is its weak point. We'll need to concentrate our attacks there."

As they prepared for battle, the Frozen Heart reacted to their presence. Ice surged from the ground, forming blizzards and icy constructs that lashed out at the group. The temperature dropped even further, and the cold became almost unbearable.

Astra raised her staff, focusing her light magic to counter the freezing storm. "We have to work together!"

Kael charged forward, his sword cutting through the icy constructs. His breath came in harsh gasps as the cold slowed his movements, but he pushed on, driving toward the heart.

Draven moved like a shadow, striking from the darkness to exploit the heart's vulnerabilities. "Focus on the core!" he called, using his magic to create openings for his companions.

Liora's magic kept them warm and strong, her light shining through the freezing storm. She healed their injuries, ensuring they could continue fighting despite the bitter cold.

Zephyr fired bursts from his energy blaster, each shot aimed at the heart's core. The cold gnawed at him, but his adventurous spirit remained strong. "We're breaking it down!"

Ethan's equipment buzzed as he coordinated their efforts. "Keep focusing on the core! It's weakening!"

Finally, with a united effort, Astra channeled all her magic into a single, powerful blast that struck the Frozen Heart directly in its core. The crystal trembled before shattering, its icy glow fading as the chamber returned to silence.

The Frozen Heart was defeated.

"We did it," Astra breathed, her voice filled with relief. "The ice's power is broken."

Kael sheathed his sword, a sense of quiet victory in his expression. "We've won. But the journey continues."

The group had conquered the Ice Caves of Glacia, but the challenges were far from over.

SCENE 4 - YEAR 3127 - DAY 078:
ICICLE CHAMBER

With the Frozen Heart shattered, the group ventured deeper into the Ice Caves, following a narrow, winding passage that led them to another chamber. The temperature had stabilized slightly, but the air was still frigid, making their every breath feel heavy.

The new chamber was even more magnificent than the last. Massive icicles, each shimmering with a faint blue light, hung from the ceiling like frozen stalactites. The walls were covered in intricate frost patterns that seemed to pulse with ancient magic. At the center of the room, suspended from the ceiling by crystalline tendrils, was the artifact they had come for—an ice crystal glowing with ethereal light.

Astra raised her staff, the glow illuminating the chamber in a soft, white light. "That's it," she whispered. "The artifact."

Kael studied the icicles, noticing how delicately they hung from the ceiling. "We'll need to be careful. One wrong move, and those things will come crashing down."

Draven's shadow magic flickered as he began examining the room for traps. "This chamber is full of magic. The artifact is protected, and we'll need to figure out how to retrieve it."

Liora placed her hands on the icy floor, feeling the magic flow through the ground. "The artifact is connected to the ice. We'll need to manipulate the elements around us to retrieve it safely."

Zephyr looked around, his eyes shining with a mix of awe and excitement. "I'm guessing this is another puzzle. Let's see if we can solve it without bringing the entire ceiling down on our heads."

Ethan, already scanning the room, synced his Universal Translator with the chamber's magic. "We'll need to align the patterns of light and ice. The answer is in the room—it's just a matter of deciphering it."

The group worked carefully, studying the shifting patterns of light that danced across the icy walls. Astra's staff glowed brighter as she focused on the alignment of the light beams, guiding them toward the central crystal.

As the group maneuvered the light beams, they saw the icicles shift ever so slightly, responding to the magic they were controlling. Kael stood on guard, ready to react at a moment's notice if the ceiling threatened to collapse.

Draven, using his shadow magic, found that certain areas of the chamber were illusions, designed to distract them.

"The real path is hidden," he said, his voice low but determined. "We need to follow the magic in the light."

With Liora's guidance and Zephyr's keen eyes for puzzles, the group carefully adjusted the light beams until they formed a perfect alignment, shining directly on the suspended artifact.

With a low hum, the ice crystal slowly descended from the ceiling, its glow intensifying as it settled into Astra's hands. The chamber pulsed with a soft, blue light, and the magic that had held the icicles in place dissipated.

Astra examined the ice crystal, feeling its power. "It holds the essence of the cold," she whispered. "With this, we can control the ice and use its magic to protect us in the trials ahead."

Kael nodded; his expression serious. "We've gained a powerful tool, but we'll need to be cautious with it."

Draven's shadow magic flickered as he prepared for the next challenge. "The artifact will help us, but we must use it wisely."

Liora's hands glowed with healing light as she touched the crystal, feeling its energy flow through her. "This will strengthen our bond. Together, we are unstoppable."

Zephyr grinned as he looked up at the now-still ceiling. "Another victory for the team! Let's keep this momentum going."

Ethan, studying the artifact, adjusted his equipment. "We'll need to analyze this further, but it will be crucial in the challenges to come."

With the ice crystal in their possession, the group prepared to leave the chamber, knowing that their journey through the Ice Caves was nearing its end—but they weren't out of danger yet.

SCENE 5 - YEAR 3127 - DAY 079: GUARDIAN'S RETURN

Just as the group began their ascent out of the Ice Caves, a familiar rumble echoed through the walls. From the shadows of the cavern, two frost giants emerged, their cold blue eyes glowing with fury. The ground shook with each of their steps, and the air turned frigid as they advanced, blocking the exit.

"They're back," Zephyr said, his grin fading. "And they don't look too happy."

Astra raised the ice crystal, its blue light pulsing as she prepared to use its power. "We'll need to use everything we've learned to defeat them."

Kael unsheathed his sword, his stance unwavering. "We took them on once; we can do it again."

Draven's shadow magic surged around him. "This time, we have the ice crystal. We can use their own power against them."

Liora's healing light glowed brightly, ready to support the group in the coming battle. "Together, we'll win this."

Ethan adjusted his equipment and quickly analyzed the frost giants' movements. "Their core is their weakness. Focus our attacks there."

The frost giants roared, their massive fists pounding the ground as they prepared to charge. The group spread out, coordinating their efforts with precision.

Astra channeled the power of the ice crystal, creating a protective barrier of frost around the group. The giants' attacks crashed against the barrier, but it held firm. "Now!" she called.

Kael dashed forward, his sword flashing as he struck at the giants' icy armor. Each blow chipped away at their defenses, but the cold gnawed at him, slowing his movements.

Draven moved like a shadow, slipping between the giants' attacks and striking at their weak points. His magic created openings for the others to exploit.

Liora's healing magic kept the group strong, her light providing warmth in the freezing battle. Zephyr, with his energy blaster, fired at the giants, his shots aimed directly at their cores.

Finally, Ethan's calculated strike revealed a critical vulnerability in the giants' armor. "There! Hit them now!"

With a final, coordinated assault, the group's combined power shattered the giants' icy forms, and they crumbled to the ground, defeated.

"We did it," Astra said, breathing heavily. "The giants are gone."

Kael sheathed his sword, a sense of accomplishment settling over him. "We're stronger than ever."

Draven nodded, his shadow magic fading. "But the journey isn't over yet."

Liora's healing light continued to shine as she tended to the group's injuries. "We're ready for whatever comes next."

Zephyr's grin returned as he looked around the frozen cavern. "That's another win for the team. Let's keep going."

Ethan adjusted his gear and nodded. "The next challenge won't be any easier, but we're prepared."

With the frost giants defeated and the ice crystal secured, the group continued their journey, knowing they had grown stronger with every challenge they faced.

SCENE 6 - YEAR 3127 - DAY 080: JOURNEY CONTINUES

The group emerged from the Ice Caves into the wintry expanse of Glacia, their faces flushed with victory despite the freezing wind that greeted them. The sky was a pale blue, and the snow stretched out in every direction, glittering in the faint sunlight.

Astra raised her staff, her heart filled with determination. "We've passed the trials of the Ice Caves, but we have much farther to go."

Kael stepped forward; his expression resolute. "We've faced every challenge head-on, and we'll continue to do so. Next, we head to the Floating Islands of Aether."

Draven's shadow magic flickered in the pale light; his readiness unwavering. "We're stronger now. We're ready for whatever lies ahead."

Liora smiled softly, her healing light pulsing gently. "We've gained new abilities and new strength. We'll use them to protect each other."

Zephyr stretched, looking out over the frozen landscape. "Another day, another adventure. I'm ready for the next one."

Ethan adjusted his equipment, syncing it to the next phase of their journey. "The ice crystal will be invaluable. We'll need it for the trials ahead."

Together, they set off toward their next destination—the Floating Islands of Aether. Their bond as a group had never been stronger, and they were ready to face the trials that awaited them.

As they walked, the wind howled behind them, carrying with it the whispers of the challenges they had conquered. They knew that the road ahead would be filled with danger, but they were prepared.

Together, they would rise to meet their destiny and challenge the darkness that threatened their world. Their epic quest continued, and nothing would stand in their way.

CHAPTER 10:

FLOATING ISLANDS OF AETHER

SCENE 1 - YEAR 3127 - DAY 081: THE ASCENSION

THE SKY STRETCHED BEFORE THEM LIKE A GREAT OCEAN, RESTLESS AND VAST, WITH SWIRLING CLOUDS SHIFTING IN HUES OF DEEP GREY AND VIBRANT BLUE. LIGHTNING FLICKERED IN THE DISTANCE, ILLUMINATING THE TOWERING FLOATING ISLANDS OF AETHER, SUSPENDED AS IF BY UNSEEN HANDS. THE ISLANDS, GREAT MASSES OF ROCK AND EARTH, HOVERED FAR ABOVE THE WORLD BELOW, CONNECTED BY FRAGILE BRIDGES OF LIGHT, PULSATING WITH AN EERIE, OTHERWORLDLY GLOW. ABOVE, THE HEAVENS ROARED WITH STORM AND FURY, THE WINDS TEARING AT THE EDGES OF THE ISLANDS, AND YET THERE WAS A STRANGE BEAUTY TO THE CHAOS. IT

WAS A PLACE WHERE THE PHYSICAL AND THE MYSTICAL COLLIDED, WHERE NATURE ITSELF SEEMED TO REBEL AND YET FOLLOW AN ANCIENT, UNKNOWN ORDER.

Astra stood at the forefront of the group; her eyes narrowed as she gazed upon the floating expanse. Her staff, ever a beacon of her connection to magic, glimmered faintly in response to the raw power around them. "The Floating Islands of Aether," she murmured, her voice tinged with awe. "A place where the elemental forces of air reign supreme. Somewhere among these islands lies the Air Elemental Artifact."

Kael, standing tall beside her, surveyed the turbulent skies with a wary eye. His hand rested lightly on the hilt of his sword, ever ready. "The air here feels dangerous," he said, his voice steady but cautious. "We can't afford to be careless. One misstep, and those winds could throw us into the abyss."

Zephyr, always one to embrace the wildness of nature, grinned despite the impending danger. "Danger? This is a paradise of adventure! Look at those islands! Suspended in the air like the greatest challenge ever laid before us." His gaze swept across the swirling skies and bridges of light with excitement.

Ethan, whose mind never stopped calculating, adjusted his equipment. His Universal Translator hummed softly, reading the shifting energies in the atmosphere.

"Zephyr's enthusiasm aside," he began, his tone calm but laced with concern, "these energy bridges are unstable. They're linked to the storms above. Cross them at the wrong moment, and we could be caught in a surge."

Draven, silent as the shadows he often slipped into, let the darkness wrap around him like a cloak, the shadows shielding him from the biting winds. His sharp eyes followed the swirling patterns of the air currents. "Not all is as it seems here," he muttered. "The air hides many things. Illusions, perhaps."

Liora, ever the beacon of calm, stood at the center of the group, her hands aglow with a soft, comforting light. Her healing magic, subtle and constant, sent warmth through them, a protection against the cold winds that sought to sap their strength. "The storms may test us, but we've faced worse," she said softly. "We must rely on each other, as always."

The group stood at the edge of their path, where the first of the energy bridges arched out before them. The air hummed with the pulse of the storm, and the path shimmered, wavering in the fierce winds. Beyond, the islands floated like ancient sentinels, waiting for the brave—or the foolish—to enter their domain.

"We press forward," Astra said, raising her staff high, its glow brighter in the growing darkness. "Together."

SCENE 2 - YEAR 3127 - DAY 082: ISLANDS OF ILLUSION

The first bridge stretched out before them, a translucent span of light that arched across a seemingly endless chasm. Below, only the vast expanse of air and swirling clouds could be seen, and the wind howled like a living creature, pulling at their cloaks and armor. Every gust threatened to send them tumbling into the depths.

Zephyr stepped forward first, his eyes gleaming with an inner confidence. The winds seemed to recognize him, parting slightly as he moved onto the bridge. His connection to the element of air was undeniable, and for a moment, it seemed as if he were walking through a familiar dance, the currents shifting in his favor. "Follow my lead," he called back, his voice rising above the roar of the storm. "The wind is tricky, but if we move in time with it, we'll cross safely."

The rest of the group followed cautiously; their eyes locked on the unstable bridge. Every step was a test of balance, of focus. The energy beneath their feet flickered with each pulse of the storm above, and the bridge vibrated with the hum of unseen forces.

Halfway across, the air seemed to shift unnaturally. A powerful gust surged from below, and from the swirling clouds, a creature of wind and lightning materialized. Its form was amorphous, ever-changing, but its eyes glowed with malevolent intent. The Wind Wraith, as ancient as the islands themselves, let out a deafening screech as it lunged at them, its body crackling with electrical energy.

Kael's sword was out in an instant, his warrior instincts kicking in. He blocked the creature's first strike, but the force of the wind nearly knocked him off balance. "We need to find a way to strike it!" he shouted over the storm.

Astra raised her staff, light magic surging forth to form a protective barrier around the group. The Wind Wraith circled them, its lightning-charged form darting in and out of the storm, too fast for a direct strike.

Draven vanished into the shadows, his form blending with the storm's dark clouds. "It's made of wind," he said, his voice barely audible over the storm. "We need to weaken its form before we can land a solid hit."

Ethan's mind raced as he analyzed the creature's movements. "It solidifies just before it strikes!" he called out. "We have to hit it when it gathers energy for an attack."

With that knowledge, the group prepared for the next assault. Zephyr manipulated the winds around them, creating pockets of calm air to trap the creature for a brief moment. When the Wind Wraith gathered itself to strike again, Kael lunged, his sword flashing through the air. His blade connected with the creature's core, and it let out a piercing scream as its form destabilized.

Astra unleashed a burst of light magic, and Liora channeled her healing energy to protect them from the creature's final surge of power. The Wraith dissipated into the storm, its energy dispersing harmlessly into the air.

The group, breathless but victorious, continued their trek across the bridge. The path ahead was treacherous, but their unity and strength had seen them through.

"Well, that was fun," Zephyr said with a grin as they reached the other side. His enthusiasm, though undimmed, was tempered by the gravity of their journey.

SCENE 3 - YEAR 3127 - DAY 083: TEMPLE OF WINDS

The path led them to the heart of the floating island, where an ancient structure stood tall against the backdrop of the swirling storm—the Temple of Winds. Its towering spires stretched into the sky; their shapes twisted by the air currents that spiraled around them. The very walls of the temple seemed alive with movement, as if the winds themselves were embedded in the stone, shifting and swirling like a living entity.

Astra approached the entrance with caution, her staff glowing brighter as they neared the source of immense magic. "The artifact is here," she said softly, her voice echoing in the vast emptiness of the temple's grand hall. "But it is guarded. The air itself is the gatekeeper."

Inside, the temple's vast corridors were lined with ancient carvings and runes, their meanings long forgotten by time. But the Universal Translators each member carried hummed to life, deciphering the cryptic symbols as they moved deeper into the temple. Ethan's device glowed brightly as he read the runes aloud.

"The winds hold the key," he said, glancing up from the translator. "We need to align the currents to open the way forward."

Zephyr stepped forward, his connection to the air already responding to the unseen forces within the temple. "Leave this to me," he said, his grin returning. "I know how the wind moves."

With that, the group began working together to manipulate the wind currents that flowed through the temple's chambers. Astra used her light magic to illuminate hidden passages, while Kael and Draven kept watch for any signs of danger. Liora's healing magic kept the group centered, her calm presence a steady anchor in the chaos of the swirling winds.

The air within the temple began to shift, responding to their efforts. Slowly, the winds aligned, and the ancient mechanism that guarded the path to the artifact began to move. A great stone door, carved with symbols of the air and sky, slid open, revealing a hidden passage that led to the heart of the temple.

"The way forward is clear," Astra said, her staff still glowing with the energy of the temple. "But we must be prepared. The true test lies ahead."

And so, with the winds at their backs and the storm still raging above, they pressed onward, deeper into the Floating Islands of Aether, where the Sky Guardian awaited.

SCENE 4 - YEAR 3127 - DAY 084:
EYE OF THE STORM

The passage led the group to a grand chamber, open to the swirling skies above. At the center of the room stood a towering altar of gleaming stone, covered in intricate carvings that depicted the ancient gods of air and sky. Suspended above the altar, in the eye of a swirling vortex of wind and lightning, hovered the Air Elemental

Artifact, a glowing crystal that pulsed with the raw energy of the storm.

But as they stepped into the chamber, the air grew heavier, thick with the weight of ancient power. The winds howled louder, and from the swirling clouds above, a massive figure began to take shape. Formed entirely from the air itself, the Sky Guardian emerged— a creature of pure elemental energy, its body constantly shifting and reforming as the winds roared around it. Its eyes, glowing like twin stars, locked onto the group with an otherworldly intelligence.

Astra gripped her staff tightly, her heart pounding in her chest. "The Sky Guardian," she whispered. "The protector of the artifact."

Kael stepped forward, his sword drawn, ready for the inevitable battle. "We've faced guardians before," he said, his voice steady. "This one will fall, just like the others."

But Zephyr, who had been the most exuberant throughout their journey, looked at the Sky Guardian with a hint of reverence. "This isn't just another foe," he said quietly. "It's the embodiment of the air, the very force we've been trying to harness."

Ethan's mind raced as he scanned the creature with his equipment, trying to find a weakness. "It's pure elemental energy," he muttered. "We can't just strike it down. We need to disrupt its connection to the winds."

Draven, his eyes narrowing as he studied the swirling form of the guardian, slipped into the shadows, waiting for the right moment to strike. "If it's connected to the air, then perhaps we can sever that connection."

Liora, ever the healer and protector, stood at the ready, her hands glowing with light as she prepared to shield the group from the oncoming storm. "We'll need to work together. This guardian is more powerful than anything we've faced before."

The Sky Guardian let out a deafening roar, the winds around it surging violently. Lightning crackled through the air as the guardian charged toward them, its massive form descending with the force of a hurricane.

Astra raised her staff, summoning a barrier of light to protect them from the initial assault. The winds battered against the barrier, threatening to tear it apart, but Astra held firm, her magic glowing brighter as she fought against the elemental fury.

Kael dashed forward, his sword gleaming in the storm's light. He swung his blade with precision, aiming for the core of the guardian, but his strikes passed through its swirling form as if cutting through air itself. "It's like trying to fight a cloud!" he growled, frustration creeping into his voice.

Draven, moving with the speed of shadows, darted around the edges of the battlefield, his daggers flashing as he sought a way to strike. "We need to disrupt its form," he called out. "It's too fast and too fluid to hit directly."

Zephyr, eyes alight with understanding, stepped forward, his arms outstretched. He called upon his connection to the air, manipulating the winds around him. "I can feel it!" he shouted over the roar of the storm. "It's drawing power from the vortex. If we can break the flow of the wind, we can weaken it!"

Ethan's equipment buzzed as he quickly recalculated their strategy. "We need to disrupt the flow of air," he confirmed. "If Zephyr can manipulate the winds, the rest of us can strike when its form becomes unstable."

With a plan in place, the group moved into action. Zephyr focused all of his energy on controlling the air currents, redirecting the flow of wind away from the Sky Guardian. Slowly, the vortex began to weaken, and the guardian's form flickered as its connection to the storm was disrupted.

Kael seized the opportunity, lunging forward with his sword. This time, his blade found purchase, striking the core of the guardian and sending a shockwave of energy through its form. The guardian howled in pain, its body destabilizing as the winds around it faltered.

Astra, her staff glowing with brilliant light, channeled her magic into a powerful blast, striking the guardian with pure elemental energy. Liora's healing light surrounded the group, protecting them from the backlash of the storm as the guardian writhed in agony.

Draven, ever the opportunist, struck from the shadows, his daggers sinking into the weakened core of the guardian. "Now!" he shouted, his voice cutting through the chaos. "While it's vulnerable!"

With a final surge of strength, the group launched their combined assault. Zephyr unleashed the full force of his air magic, tearing the winds away from the guardian. Kael's sword cut through its core, and Astra's magic shattered the last of its defenses.

The Sky Guardian let out one final, deafening roar before its form dissolved into the air, its essence scattering into the wind. The storm above began to calm, and the air around them grew still.

SCENE 5 - YEAR 3127 - DAY 085:
FINAL CHALLENGE

As the winds died down, the chamber grew quiet, and the only sound that remained was the soft hum of the Air Elemental Artifact, still hovering above the altar. The glowing crystal pulsed gently, its power no longer chaotic but serene, as if acknowledging the group's victory.

Astra stepped forward; her staff held high as she approached the altar. The air around her seemed to part, making way for her as she reached out to claim the artifact. Her fingers brushed against the surface of the crystal, and a surge of energy flowed through her, filling her with a sense of calm and clarity.

"The artifact of air," she whispered, her voice filled with reverence. "Its power is bound to the skies, to the winds that shape the world."

Kael stood beside her; his sword sheathed once more. He looked at the crystal with a mixture of respect and caution. "We've earned this victory," he said quietly. "But we can't afford to let our guard down. There are still greater challenges ahead."

Zephyr, ever the adventurer, stepped forward with a wide grin. "That was incredible!" he exclaimed; his eyes gleaming with excitement. "The way the winds moved, the way we fought together—it was like nothing I've ever experienced."

Ethan adjusted his equipment, his expression more focused than celebratory. "This artifact will be crucial in the battles to come," he said. "But we need to study it carefully. Its power is immense, and we'll need to use it wisely."

Draven, always the pragmatist, lingered in the shadows, his eyes on the swirling clouds above. "The winds have calmed," he said softly. "But the storm isn't over. We've only delayed the next challenge."

Liora's healing light surrounded the group, soothing their wounds and restoring their strength. "We're stronger now," she said, her voice gentle but firm. "We've faced the storm and come through the other side. Together."

Astra carefully lifted the artifact from its resting place, the crystal glowing softly in her hands. She could feel its connection to the air, to the winds that had once been wild and untamable. But now, the artifact's power was hers to command.

"The winds are with us," she said, her voice filled with quiet determination. "And they will guide us in the battles to come."

With the Air Elemental Artifact in their possession, the group turned to leave the chamber, their hearts filled with a renewed sense of purpose. They had faced the storm and emerged victorious, but they knew that their journey was far from over.

SCENE 6 - YEAR 3127 - DAY 086:
THE DESCENT

As the group made their way back across the floating islands, the skies had begun to clear. The storm that had once raged around them had calmed, leaving behind a peaceful, almost serene landscape. The islands, still suspended high above the world, now seemed less threatening, their bridges of light glowing softly in the fading light of day.

Zephyr, ever eager to reflect on their adventure, looked out over the horizon with a contented smile. "I think this is my favorite place so far," he said, his voice filled with wonder. "The air, the sky, the winds—it feels like home."

Astra, still holding the artifact, looked down at the glowing crystal in her hands. "The winds have accepted us," she said softly. "But we must use this power wisely. There are greater trials ahead."

Kael, always the protector, stood at the edge of the bridge, his hand resting on the hilt of his sword. "We're stronger now," he said, his voice steady. "But we must remain vigilant. The darkness still lurks ahead."

Draven, his eyes ever watchful, glanced at the shifting clouds above. "The storm may have passed," he said quietly. "But the real battle is still to come."

Ethan, his equipment buzzing softly, nodded in agreement. "The Air Elemental Artifact will give us an advantage," he said. "But we need to stay focused. There's still much we don't understand about its power."

Liora, always the calm center of the group, smiled softly as she looked around at her companions. "We've come this far together," she said, her voice filled with warmth. "And we'll continue forward, no matter what challenges lie ahead."

With the Air Elemental Artifact in their possession, and the storm behind them, the group continued their journey across the floating islands. They had faced the winds of Aether, passed the trials of the Sky Guardian, and emerged stronger than ever.

But their quest was far from over.

Together, they would face whatever challenges lay ahead, their bond unbreakable, their spirits unwavering. The skies had given them their blessing, and with the winds at their back, they pressed forward, ready to face the next chapter of their epic adventure.

CHAPTER 11:

THE SHADOW REALM

SCENE 1 - YEAR 3127 - DAY 087: ENTERING THE SHADOW REALM

THE SHADOW REALM STRETCHED BEFORE THEM, A PLACE WHERE DAY AND NIGHT BLENDED INTO ONE LONG, UNENDING TWILIGHT. DARK CLOUDS SWIRLED OVERHEAD, CASTING AN EERIE, OTHERWORLDLY HUE OVER THE LAND. THE GROUND BENEATH THEIR FEET SEEMED AS THOUGH IT HAD BEEN TWISTED BY SOME UNSEEN FORCE, WARPED AND BARREN, WITH JAGGED FORMATIONS OF STONE AND SHADOW RISING OMINOUSLY FROM THE SURFACE. THE AIR ITSELF FELT HEAVY, THICK WITH THE WEIGHT OF FOREBODING ENERGY, AS IF THE DARKNESS THAT PERVADED THIS REALM SOUGHT TO PULL THEM IN WITH EACH STEP.

Draven was the first to speak. His voice was low, reverberating through the shadows. "This is the Shadow Realm," he said, his eyes glinting with familiarity. "A place where light is scarce, and darkness reigns." The power of his own shadow magic seemed amplified here, as though the darkness of the realm called to him, welcoming him as one of its own.

Astra lifted her staff, its faint glow struggling against the oppressive dark. The light from her staff was like a fragile barrier, barely holding the encroaching gloom at bay. "This realm is powerful," she murmured. "The shadows here are alive... more than just an absence of light. We must tread carefully." Her voice was steady, but there was no mistaking the tension that lay beneath it.

Kael drew his sword, the familiar weight of the blade grounding him. His eyes swept the twisted landscape. "The darkness here is thick," he said, his voice grim. "But we've faced worse. Stay sharp." His gaze lingered on the jagged formations in the distance, sensing danger lurking in their depths.

Liora stood close, her healing light offering a faint warmth against the cold emptiness that pervaded the realm. "The darkness will try to consume us," she whispered. "We must remain strong and steadfast, relying on each other to keep the shadows at bay."

Zephyr, usually lighthearted, had a more serious air about him as he surveyed their surroundings. "The

Shadow Realm is more than just a dark place," he said thoughtfully. "It's alive, shifting, waiting for us to make a mistake. But we're prepared."

Ethan's analytical mind was already at work, scanning the environment, piecing together the threats they would face. "This realm is built to test us, to wear us down," he said. "But we've outsmarted worse, and we'll do it again here."

As they pressed forward, the landscape grew even more twisted. The ground beneath them was uneven, and the shadows around them seemed to shift and move of their own accord, stretching unnaturally across the land, defying the laws of physics. Every few steps, something in the distance would flicker, like a mirage—a glimpse of something that was not truly there.

Draven's connection to the realm deepened as they moved, his shadow magic guiding them as though the darkness itself was a path only he could read. "The shadows will play tricks on us," he warned, his voice a murmur that cut through the oppressive silence. "They'll try to confuse us, make us doubt each other. But if we stay focused, trust in each other, we can navigate through this."

Astra's staff flared a little brighter, its light cutting through the deepest of the shadows. "The light may be weak here," she said, "but it still holds power. We'll follow it."

Kael moved beside her, sword in hand, eyes sharp and focused. "Let them come," he said softly. "The darkness may be thick, but we're stronger."

With every step, the group felt the weight of the realm pressing down on them, yet their bond remained unshaken. Together, guided by Draven's shadow magic and Astra's light, they moved deeper into the heart of the Shadow Realm.

SCENE 2 - YEAR 3127 - DAY 088: SHADOW'S EMBRACE

The deeper they ventured, the more palpable the darkness became. It seemed to cling to their skin, suffocating and thick. The shadows here were no longer mere tricks of the light, but something more—something alive. The air felt colder, heavier, as if the realm itself was attempting to snuff out any glimmer of hope.

Draven led the way, his shadow magic stronger than ever, as though the realm itself was feeding him power. "The shadows here aren't just illusions," he said, his voice barely more than a whisper. "They're alive. They'll try to pull us in, try to consume us."

Astra's staff struggled against the weight of the darkness, but she stood tall. "The light may falter," she said, her voice firm, "but it won't fail. Not as long as we hold it steady." Her words were a beacon, as much for herself as for the others.

Kael tightened his grip on his sword, his muscles tense and ready. "Whatever's out there, whatever's in the shadows, it can't break us," he said, his voice determined. "We've come too far for that."

Liora's healing light pulsed softly, a reminder of the warmth they carried within them, even in this forsaken place. "There's pain here," she murmured, sensing the suffering that emanated from the very ground beneath their feet. "But we can soothe it. We can survive it."

Zephyr, though still smiling, was subdued. "The Shadow Realm is testing us," he said. "But we've got what it takes. We've always had what it takes."

Ethan adjusted his gear, his eyes flicking between the shadows that seemed to writhe and shift around them. "This place is built to make us lose focus, to play on our fears," he observed. "But if we stay sharp, we can outsmart it."

The shadows began to shift, more tangible now, creeping closer with each step. Strange shapes emerged from the darkness—creatures formed from the very essence of shadow, their movements fluid and unnatural.

Kael was the first to engage, his sword flashing in the dim light as he struck down the nearest shadow creature. The creature dissipated into a cloud of darkness, but more took its place.

Draven moved with precision, his shadow magic flaring as he countered the creatures' attacks. "They're part of the realm," he said through gritted teeth. "We can't destroy them all. But we can push through."

Liora's healing magic flared as she tended to the group, her light keeping them strong, even as the shadows sought to overwhelm them

Zephyr fired his energy blaster, each shot aimed at the core of the shadow creatures. "Keep moving!" he called. "We've got to get through this!"

Ethan, analyzing the creatures' patterns, called out, "They're drawn to our light! Use it to lure them away!"

Together, they fought through the onslaught, their combined strength pushing back the shadows. With each creature they defeated, they grew stronger, more determined.

The shadows, alive and dangerous, could not break their resolve.

SCENE 3 - YEAR 3127 - DAY 089:
RIVER OF SHADOWS

The landscape ahead began to shift, the twisted ground giving way to a dark and swirling river that cut through the desolate terrain. Its waters were black as night, reflecting no light, only rippling with an otherworldly energy that filled the air with a chilling sense of dread. The river seemed alive, as though it could devour anything that dared to cross its path.

Liora's eyes widened as she approached the edge of the river. "The souls trapped in the water..." she whispered. "I can feel their pain. Their suffering is unbearable." The cries of the lost souls could be heard faintly, just beneath the surface, their voices a chorus of sorrow and despair.

Astra raised her staff, casting a faint glow over the water's surface, but the light was swallowed almost immediately by the darkness of the river. "The River of Shadows," she said softly. "It's said to trap the souls of those who've succumbed to the darkness of this realm."

Kael grimaced as he tightened his grip on his sword. "We need to cross," he said, his voice resolute. "But I doubt this river will make it easy."

Draven stepped forward, his connection to the shadow magic here deeper than ever. "The river is alive," he said quietly. "It will try to pull us in, just as it did to those souls trapped beneath the surface. But we can cross... if we are careful and if we trust each other."

Zephyr, standing at the river's edge, stared into the churning waters. "This place gives me the creeps," he muttered. "But we've faced worse. I'm not about to let a river get the better of us."

Ethan, studying the river, spoke up. "There has to be a way across. If we can find the rhythm of the currents and the points where the darkness is weakest, we can make it."

Liora, her hands glowing softly, stepped forward. "I can create a passage," she said, her voice calm but firm. "The souls are suffering, but my light can soothe them. We'll cross on a path of light."

With slow, deliberate movements, Liora extended her hands over the river. Her healing light flowed from her fingertips, spreading across the surface of the water, creating a faintly glowing path of light that stretched from one shore to the other. The cries of the trapped souls quieted as her light reached them, their despair momentarily calmed.

"Follow the path," Liora urged. "But be quick. My light won't last forever."

Astra was the first to step onto the glowing path, her staff held high. The light flickered beneath her feet, but she pressed forward, her heart steady. "We'll cross together," she said firmly. "Stay close and keep moving."

Kael was next, his sword drawn as he moved cautiously across the bridge of light. The river surged and rippled beneath them, but the path held firm under Liora's magic. "Stay alert," he called to the others. "There's something moving beneath the surface."

As the group crossed, the dark water churned violently, and shadowy figures began to emerge from the depths. Hands of shadow reached out, clawing at the path of light, their touch cold and filled with despair.

Draven's shadow magic flared, cutting through the hands that reached for them. "The river's trying to pull us in!" he warned. "Keep moving!"

Zephyr fired his blaster into the river, each shot aimed at the shadowy figures that rose from the depths. "I don't like this!" he shouted over the roar of the water. "But we're almost there!"

Ethan, quick to analyze the shifting currents, called out instructions. "The shadows are drawn to our movement! Stay in formation and move together!"

The path of light flickered dangerously as the river's power grew, but Liora's healing magic shone brighter in response, holding the shadows at bay. Her face was strained with concentration, but she pressed on, determined to lead them safely across.

Kael slashed through a tendril of shadow that attempted to grab his ankle, his sword gleaming in the faint light. "We won't be pulled in!" he growled, pushing forward with renewed determination.

Finally, they reached the other side of the river, breathless and shaken but unbroken. Liora's light faded, and the path across the river disappeared behind them, leaving the dark waters swirling and churning once more.

Astra lowered her staff, her gaze fixed on the river. "We made it," she said, her voice filled with relief. "But the shadows won't stop here."

Draven nodded, his shadow magic still pulsing around him. "The river tried to take us," he said quietly. "But we fought back. We'll need that strength for what lies ahead."

Zephyr let out a shaky laugh. "That was close," he admitted. "But we made it. Let's hope the next challenge doesn't involve another creepy river."

Ethan adjusted his gear, his mind already racing ahead to the next obstacle. "We're not done yet," he said, his tone serious. "But we've come this far, and we'll keep going."

With the River of Shadows behind them, the group pressed on, knowing that the trials of the Shadow Realm were far from over.

SCENE 4 - YEAR 3127 - DAY 090: TOWER OF SHADOWS

The Tower of Shadows loomed ahead of them, a massive structure of black stone that rose high into the sky, its surface etched with ancient runes that pulsed faintly in the darkness. The air around the tower was thick with an almost tangible sense of dread, as if the very stones were alive with the power of the shadows that dwelled within.

Astra's staff glowed softly as they approached the tower. "This is it," she whispered. "The Tower of Shadows... a place where light struggles to exist."

Kael tightened his grip on his sword, his eyes scanning the towering structure. "This place reeks of danger," he muttered. "But we've faced worse."

Draven's shadow magic pulsed as he took a step forward, his connection to the darkness deepening with each moment. "The tower is alive with shadows," he said quietly. "They'll try to confuse us, mislead us. We must stay focused."

Liora stood at the center of the group, her healing light casting a warm glow around them. "The shadows will test us," she said softly. "But we are stronger together."

Zephyr studied the tower, his usual grin replaced by a thoughtful expression. "This is going to be tricky," he mused. "But we've got the skills to make it through."

Ethan, always the strategist, was already analyzing the structure. "There will be traps," he said, his voice steady. "But we can outsmart them if we stay sharp."

As they entered the tower, the darkness closed in around them, oppressive and heavy. The walls seemed to shift and move, as if the very stones were alive, and the shadows stretched out, reaching for them with unseen hands.

Draven's shadow magic flared as he guided them, his voice steady. "The shadows will try to consume us," he said. "But we can push through. Trust in the light."

Astra's staff glowed brighter, her light pushing back the darkness as they moved deeper into the tower. "The light may be weak here," she said, "but it's still powerful. We will not falter."

Kael followed closely behind; his sword ready. "Whatever the shadows throw at us," he said grimly, "we will not break."

With every step, the darkness grew thicker, and the tower's traps began to spring. Shadowy figures emerged from the walls; ancient traps activated by their presence. But the group moved as one, their strength and unity pushing them forward, ever closer to the heart of the tower.

SCENE 5 - YEAR 3127 - DAY 091: SHADOW'S CORE

As they ascended the twisting, shadow-filled corridors of the Tower of Shadows, the air grew heavier with the weight of ancient magic. The oppressive darkness was suffocating, pressing in on the group from all sides, yet they pressed on with unshaken resolve. At the heart of the tower, they finally came upon the Shadow's Core—a swirling vortex of pure darkness, suspended in the air above an ancient altar. Its presence filled the chamber with a palpable sense of dread.

The chamber itself was vast, its walls etched with runes that pulsed with faint light. The ground was cold beneath their feet, slick as if covered in frost, and the very air hummed with the power of the shadows.

Astra lifted her staff, the light struggling to pierce through the dense darkness that surrounded the

Shadow's Core. "This is it," she whispered. "The source of the shadows' power. The artifact we seek lies within."

Kael stepped forward, his sword gleaming faintly in the dim light. "If we retrieve it, the balance of power here will shift in our favor," he said grimly. "But the shadows won't let us take it without a fight."

Draven's eyes glowed with dark energy as he stared into the swirling vortex. His connection to the shadows was stronger here than ever before, yet it took every ounce of his will to resist being drawn into the Core's pull. "We must be careful," he murmured. "The shadows are alive here, and they will not give up their power easily."

Liora, her healing light shining gently in the gloom, sensed the danger in the air. "The Core is feeding off the despair of this realm," she said softly. "It will try to overwhelm us, but we must stand strong."

Zephyr glanced warily at the swirling mass of darkness. "Something tells me this is going to get a lot worse before it gets better," he said, gripping his blaster tightly.

Ethan adjusted his gear, his mind already racing to devise a plan. "The Core is unstable," he observed. "If we disrupt it too much, we could trigger a chain reaction that destroys this entire tower—and us along with it."

Draven stepped forward, his voice steady despite the growing tension. "I'll control the shadows," he said. "I can guide them, calm the chaos within the Core. But I'll need help."

Astra nodded, her staff glowing brighter. "I'll lend my light to hold back the darkness."

With a deep breath, Draven extended his hands toward the swirling vortex, his shadow magic flaring as he reached into the heart of the Core. The shadows responded instantly, lashing out with tendrils of dark energy that twisted and coiled toward him. But Draven remained calm, his focus unwavering as he bent the shadows to his will, channeling their chaotic energy into a controlled flow.

Astra stepped beside him; her staff held high as she unleashed a steady beam of light into the Core. The two forces—light and shadow—met in the center of the chamber, clashing but not warring, forming a delicate balance that held the Core's destructive power at bay.

Kael, ever vigilant, stood guard, his sword ready to strike down any threats that might arise from the shadows. "Stay sharp," he warned the others. "If anything goes wrong, we'll need to act fast."

Liora, her light gentle but resolute, focused on maintaining the group's strength. The strain of controlling such immense power was taking its toll on Draven and Astra, but her healing magic kept them steady, preventing the darkness from seeping into their souls.

Zephyr's grin had faded, replaced by grim determination as he scanned the chamber for signs of danger. "We've got this," he muttered to himself, his blaster humming in his hands. "Just a little longer..."

The Core pulsed violently, sending ripples of dark energy through the room, but Draven and Astra held firm. Slowly, the vortex began to shrink, its wild, chaotic energy calming as the forces of light and shadow wove together.

Ethan, standing at the edge of the altar, analyzed the runes that lined the walls of the chamber. "The Core's power is bound to these ancient symbols," he said. "If we can decipher them, we might be able to stabilize the Core and extract the artifact without destroying the tower."

"Then let's move," Kael urged. "We don't have much time."

As Ethan worked to unravel the ancient runes, Astra and Draven continued to control the flow of energy from the Core. Sweat dripped from their brows, but they did not falter. The balance between light and shadow was fragile, yet they held it steady with sheer force of will.

At last, the Core shrank to a manageable size, revealing its heart—a small, crystalline sphere that pulsed with a soft, dark glow. It hovered in the center of the chamber, suspended in the air by the remnants of the vortex's energy.

Astra reached out cautiously, her hand trembling as she approached the sphere. "This is it," she whispered. "The Shadow's Core. The artifact that controls the very essence of darkness."

Draven nodded; his voice quiet but resolute. "It's ours now. But we must use it wisely."

With great care, Astra wrapped her fingers around the crystalline sphere. The moment she touched it, a surge of energy coursed through her, connecting her to the shadows that had once threatened to overwhelm them. But instead of fear, she felt a deep sense of understanding—of the balance between light and darkness that existed in all things.

"The artifact is in our hands," Astra said, turning to the group. "The power of the shadows now belongs to us."

Kael sheathed his sword, his expression serious but relieved. "We've passed the trials of the tower," he said. "But we're not out of danger yet."

Draven's shadow magic flared one last time as he stabilized the remnants of the vortex. "The shadows may be calmed for now," he said, "but the forces of darkness are always waiting."

Zephyr let out a long breath, his grin returning as he slung his blaster over his shoulder. "Another win for the good guys," he said. "Now let's get out of here before this place collapses on us."

Ethan, his eyes still on the runes, nodded in agreement. "The tower is unstable," he said. "We need to move, fast."

With the Shadow's Core safely in their possession, the group turned and made their way toward the exit of the tower, knowing that the final battle with the forces of darkness was still to come.

SCENE 6 - YEAR 3127 - DAY 092: SHADOW'S FALL

As they descended the Tower of Shadows, the atmosphere around them grew more oppressive, as though the tower itself sensed that its power was slipping away. The walls trembled, and the air hummed with dark energy, growing increasingly unstable with each step they took.

The group moved quickly, knowing that time was against them. But as they neared the tower's exit, a deep, resonant sound echoed through the air—a sound that filled the chamber with a sense of impending doom.

Out of the very shadows themselves emerged a massive entity, its form shifting and writhing like a living storm of darkness. It towered above them, its glowing red eyes fixed on the group with a hunger that sent chills down their spines.

Kael drew his sword in an instant, his muscles tensing for the fight ahead. "It's not going to let us leave without a fight," he said grimly.

Astra raised her staff, the Shadow's Core glowing faintly in her hand. "The shadow entity is trying to reclaim the artifact," she said. "But we won't let it."

Draven's shadow magic flared as he stepped forward. "This creature is born of the shadows," he said quietly. "But it can be defeated. We just need to hit its core."

Zephyr's blaster hummed as he prepared to fire. "Let's take it down!"

Ethan quickly analyzed the creature, his eyes darting over its shifting form. "Aim for the center!" he shouted. "That's where its power is concentrated!"

Liora stood at the ready, her healing light casting a warm glow over the group. "We'll need to stay strong," she said softly. "This will be our greatest challenge yet."

With a deafening roar, the shadow entity lunged at them, its massive arms made of pure darkness reaching out to crush them. But Kael was ready, his sword flashing as he met the creature's attack head-on, his blade slicing through the shadowy tendrils.

Draven's shadow magic surged as he struck from the darkness, his attacks aimed directly at the creature's core. "We can't let it gain the upper hand!" he called out. "Keep pushing forward!"

Astra raised the Shadow's Core high, its dark light radiating out in all directions. "The power of the shadows is ours now!" she shouted. "We will not be defeated!"

Zephyr fired shot after shot at the creature, each blast hitting its core with precision. "This thing's tough," he muttered. "But we've got it on the ropes!"

Liora's healing light shone brightly, keeping the group strong even as the creature's attacks grew more frenzied. "Stay focused!" she called. "We're almost there!"

With one final, coordinated effort, the group unleashed their combined power on the creature, striking its core with all the strength they had left. The shadow entity let out a piercing scream as its form began to unravel, the dark energy that had sustained it dissipating into the air.

Finally, with a deafening explosion of light and shadow, the creature was defeated, its form disintegrating into nothingness.

The group stood victorious, their breaths coming in ragged gasps as they surveyed the aftermath of the battle.

"We did it," Astra said, her voice filled with relief. "The shadow entity is defeated. Now we can leave this place."

Kael sheathed his sword, his expression one of quiet satisfaction. "We've passed the final trial," he said. "The tower is behind us, and the Shadow's Core is ours."

Draven's shadow magic flickered one last time as he surveyed the quieted tower. "The darkness is calmed," he said quietly. "For now."

Zephyr let out a long breath, his grin returning as he slung his blaster over his shoulder. "That was one heck of a fight," he said. "But we came out on top."

Ethan adjusted his equipment, his mind already focused on the challenges ahead. "The Shadow's Core will be crucial in the battles to come," he said. "We'll need to use it wisely."

Liora's healing light shone softly as she tended to the group's injuries. "We're stronger now," she said gently. "We're ready for whatever lies ahead."

With the Tower of Shadows behind them, the group set out on the next leg of their journey. They had overcome the trials of the Shadow Realm, but they knew that the greatest battles were still to come.

Together, they would face whatever darkness lay ahead, their hearts united in their quest to protect their world from the forces of evil.

CHAPTER 12:

THE RETURN TO LUMORA

SCENE 1 - YEAR 3127, DAY 093: JOURNEY HOME

THE LONG ROAD BACK TO LUMORA STRETCHED BEFORE THE GROUP LIKE A WINDING TRAIL THROUGH THE MISTS OF MEMORY. THE LANDS THEY TRAVERSED NOW BORE SCARS FROM THE BATTLES THEY HAD FOUGHT, THE CONFLICTS THEY HAD ENDURED. THE AIR ITSELF SEEMED TO HUM WITH THE POWER OF THE ARTIFACTS THEY CARRIED, AS IF THE VERY WORLD AROUND THEM COULD SENSE THE MAGNITUDE OF THEIR TASK. EVERY STEP THEY TOOK REVERBERATED WITH PURPOSE, THE WEIGHT OF THEIR JOURNEY SETTLING UPON THEIR SHOULDERS LIKE AN INVISIBLE MANTLE.

Astra led the way, her staff glowing softly, a beacon against the twilight that seemed to cloak the land in an ever-present gloom. Her face was calm, yet her eyes betrayed the storm of thoughts that swirled within her mind. "We are nearing the end," she said quietly, as though speaking more to herself than to the others. "But it is not over yet. Our greatest trial still lies ahead."

Beside her, Kael walked with a deliberate pace, his sword sheathed at his back, his gaze ever-watchful. "We've faced danger at every turn," he replied, his voice steady. "But with each battle, we've grown stronger. Serath knows we are coming, but we will be ready."

Draven moved like a shadow within the shadows, his steps nearly silent as his connection to the darkness deepened with every passing moment. "Serath's influence lingers here," he said, his voice low. "I can feel it in the very air. The darkness is not gone—it waits for us ahead. We must be prepared for anything."

Liora's light was a comforting presence, her healing magic a quiet balm that eased the tension in the group. "We've healed many wounds along this journey," she said softly, "but the final healing will come only after the battle is won. Our strength lies in our unity. We must hold fast to each other."

Zephyr's usual lighthearted grin was absent, replaced by a look of intense focus. He adjusted the artifacts hanging from his belt, their weight a reminder of the power they now wielded. "We're getting close," he said, his voice filled with quiet determination. "Closer than we've ever been. This isn't the end, but we'll finish what we started."

Ethan brought up the rear, his equipment softly humming as it scanned the landscape for threats. His mind raced, calculating strategies and possibilities for the final confrontation. "We've gathered the tools we need," he said, his tone analytical. "Now it's just a matter of using them to their full potential. Serath won't stand a chance."

As they pressed onward, remnants of Serath's dark forces emerged from the shadows—creatures twisted by the darkness, their forms barely recognizable. But each time, the group stood firm, dispatching the creatures with the skill and precision they had honed throughout their journey. The artifacts glowed brightly as they were wielded in battle, the combined power of the group pushing back the shadows that sought to impede their progress.

The familiar landscape of Lumora began to take shape in the distance, its towering spires standing like sentinels over the horizon. But as they drew nearer, the tension in the air grew thick with anticipation. Each step forward felt like a march toward destiny, toward the final test that would decide the fate of the world.

SCENE 2 - YEAR 3127 - DAY 094:
FINAL TEST

The spires of Lumora gleamed in the fading light, their ethereal glow visible even from miles away. The sight filled the group with both hope and dread—a reminder that their journey was coming to an end, but also a signal that the final battle was upon them. As if in answer to their approach, the sky above began to darken, swirling clouds gathering overhead like a storm brewing in the distance.

Kael's hand instinctively went to the hilt of his sword, his eyes narrowing as he scanned the horizon. "Something's coming," he muttered, his voice tense with anticipation. "We're not alone."

Draven's shadow magic flared; his senses attuned to the darkness that crept ever closer. "It's Serath's doing," he said quietly. "He's sent something powerful to stop us."

Astra raised her staff, its light growing brighter in response to the encroaching gloom. "Whatever it is, we will face it together," she said, her voice steady and resolute. "We've come too far to be turned back now."

The ground beneath their feet trembled as a massive figure materialized from the shadows ahead—a creature formed entirely of darkness, its eyes glowing with a malevolent light. Its presence filled the air with a palpable sense of dread, as if the very essence of the Shadow Realm had been given physical form.

"You will go no further," the creature hissed, its voice a haunting chorus of whispers that echoed in their minds. "Serath commands it."

Kael was the first to move, his sword gleaming as he charged at the entity, his strikes swift and deadly. Each blow he landed was guided by the power of the Eternal One, forcing the creature to recoil as its dark form flickered and shifted.

Draven darted through the shadows, his magic weaving through the darkness with precision. His strikes were aimed at the entity's core, each one weakening the creature's hold on the physical realm. "It's vulnerable at the heart," he called to the others. "Strike there!"

Liora's light shone brightly, a beacon of hope amidst the swirling darkness. She moved with purpose, her healing magic counteracting the corrupting influence of the creature. "Stay strong!" she urged, her light keeping the group focused and resilient.

Zephyr's energy blaster hummed as he fired shot after shot at the creature's core, his usual bravado replaced with grim determination. "We've got this," he muttered, more to himself than anyone else. "Just a little more."

Ethan adjusted his equipment, his mind working furiously as he analyzed the creature's movements. "It's losing stability!" he shouted. "Keep pressing!"

With a final, powerful strike, Astra channeled all of her magic into a beam of light that pierced the creature's core. The entity let out a deafening roar, its form shattering into fragments of darkness that dissipated into the air. The ground fell silent once more, the oppressive weight of the darkness lifting as the creature was defeated.

Breathless but victorious, the group stood amidst the fading shadows, their faces filled with relief and exhaustion. They had passed the final test.

SCENE 3 - YEAR 3127 - DAY 095:
THE REUNION

The towering gates of Lumora loomed ahead, their golden surfaces gleaming like a beacon of hope. As the group approached, a wave of emotion swept over them, a mixture of relief and anticipation. This city had been their starting point, and now, it would serve as the gathering place for the final battle.

Astra slowed her pace, her gaze fixed on the gates as memories of their journey flooded her mind. "We're home," she whispered, her voice thick with emotion. "But it's not over yet."

Kael placed a reassuring hand on her shoulder, his expression softened by the familiar sight of the city. "We've come this far," he said quietly. "We're ready for what comes next."

Draven's eyes glowed faintly as the shadows around him shifted, lighter than before. "The darkness still lingers," he murmured, "but its power is waning. Lumora's light is strong—it always has been."

Liora's gentle smile brightened the atmosphere. "Lumora has always been a place of healing," she said, her voice warm. "And now, it will be the place where we gather our strength for the final battle."

As they passed through the gates, the people of Lumora greeted them with open arms, their faces filled with hope and gratitude. Word of the group's journey had spread, and now, they were welcomed as heroes returning from a long and dangerous quest.

Familiar faces emerged from the crowd, rushing to greet them. Old friends, allies, and companions surrounded them, and for a moment, the weight of their mission lifted as they reveled in the joy of reunion.

But even in the midst of celebration, they knew that the final confrontation with Serath loomed ahead, and their brief respite would soon give way to battle once more.

SCENE 4 - YEAR 3127 - DAY 096: GATHERING OF ALLIES

The following days in Lumora were marked by a flurry of activity. Messages were sent far and wide, calling upon allies from every corner of the realm. The group knew that defeating Serath would require more than just their strength—it would take the combined might of every race and faction that stood against the darkness.

The grand hall of Lumora became the heart of the preparations. Leaders from across the land, warriors, mages, and strategists alike gathered to lend their support. The air buzzed with anticipation as each ally pledged their forces to the cause, their voices filled with determination.

Astra stood at the center of the room, her staff glowing softly with the light of the artifacts. "We have come far," she said, addressing the assembled allies. "The darkness we face is unlike any we have encountered before, but with the power of the Eternal One and the unity we have forged, we can overcome it. Together, we will stand against Serath and end his reign."

Kael stepped forward, his gaze sweeping across the room. "This battle will not be easy," he said, his voice steady. "Serath has amassed power beyond imagination, but we have something he does not—hope. We fight not only for survival but for the light that will outlast the darkness. We will stand together, and we will win."

Draven's presence in the hall was a quiet one, but his words carried weight. "I know the shadows," he said softly, his eyes dark with the knowledge of the enemy they faced. "Serath's power thrives in fear and division. But fear will not break us, and division will not weaken us. The darkness will falter under the light we carry within."

Liora's healing aura radiated out as she spoke, her voice filled with calm assurance. "We fight for the wounded, the lost, and those who have suffered under the weight of Serath's corruption. Healing will come—both to the land and to its people. But we must first defeat the darkness at its core."

Zephyr's usual light-hearted grin returned as he stepped forward, addressing the room with his characteristic confidence. "We've fought long and hard to get here," he said with a laugh. "And Serath's about to realize that he messed with the wrong team. Let's give him a fight he'll never forget!"

Ethan, ever the strategist, spoke next, his voice measured and thoughtful. "We've gathered the artifacts, studied the enemy, and prepared ourselves for this moment. Now, it's time to act. Every faction, every warrior in this room, is a vital piece of the puzzle. Together, we will strike where Serath is weakest and end his reign of terror once and for all."

As the allies pledged their support, the grand hall of Lumora was filled with a sense of unity and purpose. Warriors from the Ferron lands, mages from the Sylvari realms, navigators from Aether, and even shadow-wielders like Draven—each faction stood together, united in their shared cause.

The leader of the Ferron warriors, a tall and imposing figure, stepped forward. "We stand with Lumora and the Eternal One," he said, his voice strong. "Our swords will strike against the darkness, and we will not falter."

The Sylvari mages, their robes shimmering with ethereal light, raised their hands in a gesture of solidarity. "The magic of the Sylvari will weave through the battlefield like light through shadow," their leader declared. "We fight for the Eternal One, and for the restoration of balance."

The Aetherian navigators, known for their skills in guiding through the most treacherous of realms, also pledged their aid. "We have traversed the darkest of skies," their leader said, "and we will guide the armies of Lumora to victory."

With each pledge of allegiance, the sense of anticipation grew. The allies of Lumora were ready. Plans were laid out, strategies formed, and every warrior, mage, and leader prepared for the final confrontation with Serath.

SCENE 5 - YEAR 3127 - DAY 097: CALM BEFORE THE STORM

With the preparations complete and the forces of Lumora gathered, the city itself seemed to hold its breath. There was a palpable stillness in the air, a calm before the storm that would soon engulf them all. The final battle was imminent, and for the first time in days, the group allowed themselves a moment of peace.

Astra found herself in the gardens of Lumora, a quiet place where the warmth of the sun filtered through the trees and the sound of birdsong filled the air. She sat on a stone bench, her staff resting beside her, and closed her eyes. The light of the Eternal One pulsed gently within her, a reminder of the hope she carried.

Kael joined her, his armor gleaming in the sunlight. He sat beside her; his expression thoughtful. "Are you ready?" he asked quietly.

Astra opened her eyes and nodded. "I'm ready," she said. "We've faced so much already, and we've grown stronger with each challenge. We'll face this together."

Draven appeared as if from the shadows themselves, his presence calm and steady. "The darkness is still out there," he said softly, "but it doesn't frighten me. We've faced worse, and we will prevail."

Liora arrived soon after, her healing light radiating from her like a gentle glow. "We've healed many wounds along the way," she said, her voice tender. "But the final healing comes after the battle. Until then, we stay united in purpose and heart."

Zephyr's infectious energy returned as he approached, his grin wide. "This is it!" he exclaimed. "The final stretch. Let's make it count."

Ethan stood nearby; his gaze fixed on the horizon. "The plan is set," he said thoughtfully. "Everything is in place. All that's left is the execution."

For a brief moment, the group sat together, basking in the stillness. They knew what lay ahead, but for now, they allowed themselves to reflect on how far they had come.

"We've come so far," Astra said quietly, her voice filled with emotion. "And no matter what happens, I'm grateful for all of you."

Kael nodded; his expression serious. "We've faced danger at every turn," he said. "But we've done it together. That's what will see us through."

Draven's shadow magic flared slightly as he prepared for the final battle. "The darkness is strong," he said, "but we are stronger."

Liora's light glowed softly, her presence a calming force. "We'll see this through," she said. "Together."

Zephyr laughed; his excitement palpable. "Serath won't know what hit him," he said with a grin. "Let's get ready to finish this."

As they sat together, the sense of calm deepened. They knew that the storm was coming, but for now, they found strength in their unity, in the bonds they had forged along the way.

SCENE 6 - YEAR 3127 - DAY 098:
FINAL MARCH

The time for battle had come.

The allies of Lumora assembled, their banners flying high, the air filled with the sound of marching feet and the clang of weapons being readied. The final confrontation with Serath awaited them, and every warrior, mage, and leader knew that this battle would decide the fate of their world.

Astra led the way, her staff glowing with the light of the artifacts. "This is it," she said, her voice firm. "The final battle."

Kael walked beside her, his sword gleaming. "We've come so far," he said. "And we're ready."

Draven's shadow magic pulsed around him as he walked in step with the group. "The darkness will not win," he said. "We'll face it together."

Liora's healing light shone brightly as she moved forward with the group. "We've healed many wounds," she said softly. "But the final healing is yet to come."

Zephyr's grin was focused, his determination clear. "We're close," he said. "Let's finish what we started."

Ethan, ever the strategist, brought up the rear, his equipment softly humming as it scanned the surroundings. "Serath won't stand a chance," he said. "We've planned for everything."

As the army of Lumora marched toward the battlefield, a sense of anticipation filled the air. They had come so far, faced so many challenges, and now, they were ready to see their mission through to the end. The land ahead was dark and desolate, a reflection of Serath's influence, but the light of Lumora shone brightly behind them, a beacon of hope and strength.

The final battle was upon them.

With every step, they moved closer to destiny, to the moment that would determine the fate of their world. Together, they would stand against the darkness and challenge Serath in the ultimate confrontation.

And together, they would rise to meet their destiny.

CHAPTER 13:

BATTLE FOR THE UNIVERSE

SCENE 1 - YEAR 3127 - DAY 099: FINAL CONFRONTATION

THE BATTLEFIELD LAY BEFORE THEM, A VAST, BROKEN LANDSCAPE, MARRED BY THE WAR THAT WAS ABOUT TO UNFOLD—A WAR FOR THE FATE OF EVERYTHING THEY KNEW AND CHERISHED. THE GROUND CRACKED BENEATH THEIR FEET AS IF THE VERY EARTH GROANED IN ANTICIPATION OF THE COMING STORM. THE SKY, ONCE OPEN AND ENDLESS, NOW CHURNED WITH DENSE CLOUDS OF INKY BLACKNESS. FORKS OF VIOLET LIGHTNING CLAWED THROUGH THE HEAVENS, ILLUMINATING THE BATTLEFIELD IN QUICK, HAUNTING FLASHES THAT THREW THE JAGGED TERRAIN INTO SHARP RELIEF.

Astra took a deep breath, feeling the weight of the moment settle upon her shoulders. Her staff pulsed with the gathered power of the artifacts they had painstakingly collected, each one a fragment of the Eternal One's divine power. The glow from her staff cast long shadows around her, and as she lifted it, her companions drew nearer. Kael, his sword strapped to his back, his gaze fixed firmly on the horizon. Draven, ever the shadow, stood slightly apart, his dark robes blending with the preternatural gloom. Liora's gentle light flickered at the edges, the glow of her healing magic a constant reminder of her vital role in this coming battle. Zephyr's ever-present grin was gone now, replaced by a look of determined focus as he checked his energy blaster. And Ethan—ever the strategist—stood at the rear, analyzing, calculating.

The forces of Lumora, rallied by their leadership, formed ranks behind them. Warriors from every corner of their world had answered the call, united by the belief that the Eternal One's light would not fail them. Shields were raised, weapons gripped tightly, and a quiet tension hummed in the air. Despite their numbers, a deep silence lingered over the field, as if all creation was holding its breath.

Across the plain, Serath's dark army had amassed. They were a horrifying sight—a teeming, writhing mass of corrupted creatures. Some twisted and malformed, others shadowy and formless. Their glowing eyes pierced the murk like distant stars, but where stars brought hope, these glimmers brought only dread. At the center of this nightmarish assembly stood Serath himself—a towering figure of pure darkness, his form shifting and indistinct. His presence devoured the light, casting an oppressive pall over the entire battlefield.

Astra raised her staff high, her voice cutting through the silence like a clarion call. "This is our moment," she declared, her words carrying with them the weight of their journey, the weight of all they had sacrificed. "We fight for the universe itself, for every life, every soul, every hope. Let the Eternal One's light guide us to victory!"

A deafening roar rose up from their forces, the collective cry of those who would not yield, who would fight until their last breath. With a clash of steel and the blaze of magic, the armies of Lumora surged forward, their ranks meeting Serath's forces in an explosion of violence and fury. The ground trembled with the impact, and the sounds of battle—screams, the clash of weapons, the pulse of magic—filled the air.

Kael was the first into the fray, his sword a beacon of light as he cleaved through the twisted creatures that swarmed him. His movements were precise, each strike honed by years of training and bolstered by his faith in the Eternal One. His blade seemed to sing as it met flesh and shadow alike, cutting down the enemy with righteous fury. But for every beast he felled, two more seemed to rise in its place.

Draven moved like a ghost, his shadow magic weaving through the battlefield. He slipped in and out of sight, his form dissolving into the shadows only to reappear behind his enemies, striking with deadly precision. The darkness was his domain, but here, it fought him at every turn. Serath's influence twisted even the shadows, but Draven, with his mastery, bent them to his will. His attacks were swift and unrelenting, cutting down Serath's minions with ruthless efficiency.

Liora was a beacon of hope amidst the chaos, her healing light flaring as she moved through the battlefield. Where her light touched, wounds closed, and strength returned. Her magic was a lifeline to the soldiers who fought beside her, and though the battle raged, her presence was a calming, strengthening force.

Zephyr's energy blaster roared with each pull of the trigger, his shots precise, every blast aimed at the heart of the enemy. His eyes, usually filled with playful mischief, were now steely and focused. The battlefield was no place for his usual humor—here, only determination mattered.

Ethan, at the rear, worked furiously, his equipment buzzing as it analyzed the battlefield. He directed the group's movements with cold precision, ensuring they stayed one step ahead of Serath's horde. His mind raced as he calculated the best way to break through the enemy lines.

But Serath's army was relentless. For every creature they defeated, more surged forward, and the sheer number began to weigh on the group. Even as they fought with everything they had, exhaustion was beginning to set in.

Astra gritted her teeth, her grip on her staff tightening as she felt the strain of the artifacts' power. "We need to find Serath," she said, her voice hoarse from the effort of maintaining the flow of magic. "He's the source of this darkness. If we can stop him, the rest will fall."

Kael, covered in the blood of his enemies, nodded. "We press forward," he growled. "We don't stop until we find him."

And so, with renewed determination, they pushed deeper into the heart of the battlefield. Each step was a struggle, each strike felt heavier, but they moved as one, cutting a path through the endless tide of darkness.

SCENE 2 - YEAR 3127 - DAY 099: CLASH OF TITANS

The very air seemed to grow thicker as Serath stepped forward, his presence pulling the darkness around him like a shroud. The battlefield trembled beneath the weight of his power, and for a moment, time seemed to slow. His dark form towered above them, his eyes gleaming with cold malevolence. His voice, when he spoke, was a low, resonant growl that echoed through the souls of all who heard it.

"Fools," he hissed, his words dripping with disdain. "Did you think you could stand against me? I have woven the fabric of darkness itself. The Eternal One has no power here. Your light will be extinguished."

He raised his hand, and with a casual flick of his wrist, sent a wave of dark energy rippling across the battlefield. The shockwave hit the armies of Lumora with the force of a hurricane, scattering their ranks, throwing soldiers and creatures alike into the air as if they were nothing more than leaves caught in a storm. The ground buckled and cracked, splitting open as Serath's power coursed through it.

Astra barely managed to remain standing, her staff glowing fiercely as she struggled to counter the darkness with the power of the artifacts. "We will not let you destroy everything we've fought for," she shouted, though her voice wavered under the immense pressure of Serath's assault.

Kael charged forward, his sword blazing with the light of the Eternal One. He met Serath head-on, their weapons clashing with a sound like thunder. The force of the impact sent shockwaves rippling through the earth, and the two warriors stood locked in combat, light and darkness swirling around them in a violent dance.

But Serath was no ordinary foe. His mastery of darkness was absolute, and he wielded it with devastating precision. He moved with an unnatural speed, his dark energy meeting Kael's strikes with ease. Each time Kael's blade came down, Serath was there, blocking, countering, his movements fluid and effortless.

Draven joined the fray, his shadow magic flaring as he darted in from the side, looking for an opening. He struck at Serath's flanks, his attacks precise and calculated, but Serath was ready. With a flick of his wrist, Serath sent a pulse of dark energy that countered Draven's magic, throwing him back. Draven landed hard, the breath knocked from his lungs, but he quickly recovered, his eyes narrowing with determination.

"We need to find a weakness," Ethan called from the rear, his equipment buzzing as he frantically searched for any sign of vulnerability in Serath's defenses. "We can't keep this up forever!"

Zephyr fired his energy blaster in rapid succession, each shot aimed at Serath's core, but the dark lord's shield absorbed the blasts with ease. "We're not hitting him hard enough," Zephyr growled through gritted teeth. "We need to hit him where it hurts."

Liora, her healing light burning brightly, rushed to aid the wounded, her magic keeping the group strong even as they struggled against the overwhelming power of their foe. "We won't be defeated by darkness," she said softly, her voice steady despite the chaos around her. "The Eternal One is with us."

The battle between the group and Serath was a brutal clash of titanic forces, each side pouring their strength into the fight. The air crackled with energy, and the ground shook beneath their feet as light and darkness collided in a battle that would decide the fate of the universe.

SCENE 3 - YEAR 3127 - DAY 099: POWER OF THE ETERNAL ONE

The clash between light and darkness raged on, but as the battle reached its fevered pitch, Astra felt something—a presence, warm and familiar, as though a gentle hand had been placed on her shoulder. It was the Eternal One. His power surged through her, filling her with a clarity she had never felt before. The artifacts pulsed in response, resonating with the divine presence that now infused the air around them.

Astra closed her eyes for a brief moment, allowing the Eternal One's guidance to wash over her. In her mind's eye, she saw the path forward: the artifacts, when combined, would create a beacon of pure, unassailable light. This was the key to stopping Serath, the only way to dispel the darkness that threatened to consume everything.

Her eyes flew open, burning with new resolve. "The artifacts!" she shouted to her companions. "We need to activate them together—their combined power is the only way to defeat Serath!"

Kael, Draven, Zephyr, Liora, and Ethan exchanged glances, each of them understanding the gravity of the moment. There was no hesitation. They moved swiftly, forming a protective circle around Astra as she raised her staff high above her head, the light of the artifacts blazing like a newborn sun.

The power of the Eternal One coursed through them, and the artifacts began to glow brighter than ever before. Their individual lights, each representative of different facets of the Eternal One's power, coalesced into a single, radiant beam that pierced the darkened sky. The ground beneath their feet trembled, and the swirling darkness that had once seemed impenetrable now began to retreat in the face of this divine light.

Serath hissed in fury, recoiling from the light as though it burned him. His form flickered, the shadows that made up his body writhing and shifting as the power of the Eternal One began to weaken him.

"No!" Serath roared, his voice filled with rage and desperation. "This is not possible! I will not be defeated by the likes of you!"

The ground beneath them continued to tremble as the light grew stronger, pushing back against the darkness that clung to Serath. The very fabric of the battlefield seemed to shift as the power of the Eternal One filled the air, a tangible force that pressed against the malevolent darkness that had dominated for so long.

Serath raised his hands, summoning all of his remaining strength as he attempted to fight back. Waves of dark energy erupted from him, crashing against the group's defenses with incredible force. The ground cracked and split beneath the strain, the very air around them thick with the oppressive weight of Serath's power. But the group stood firm, their bond unbreakable, their determination unwavering.

Astra's voice rang out, filled with the strength of the Eternal One. "The darkness cannot win. Not here. Not now. The light of the Eternal One will always prevail!"

With a final surge of energy, the combined power of the artifacts reached its peak. The light that poured from Astra's staff was blinding, its purity absolute. It spread across the battlefield, washing over the landscape like a tidal wave. The creatures of darkness shrieked in agony as the light burned them away, their forms disintegrating into nothingness.

Serath staggered, his body trembling as the light engulfed him. His form began to unravel, the shadows that made up his body breaking apart under the force of the Eternal One's power. Still, he fought, his eyes blazing with fury as he clung desperately to his dark magic.

But it was futile. The light had pierced the heart of his power, and there was no escape.

SCENE 4 - YEAR 3127 - DAY 099: FINAL SACRIFICE

As the battle raged on, it became clear that, despite the weakening of Serath, his darkness still lingered. His power was vast, ancient, and even with the artifacts, it wasn't enough to fully extinguish him. The group could feel the weight of their efforts bearing down on them, exhaustion creeping in as the strain of holding the light became unbearable.

And then Kael, always the steadfast warrior, realized what must be done. His heart sank, but he knew—this was the moment he had been prepared for since the beginning of their journey. The artifacts were powerful, but to unlock their true potential, they needed a conduit—a sacrifice. Only then could they release the full might of the Eternal One's light.

"There's no other way," Kael murmured, his voice low but resolute. His hand tightened on the hilt of his sword as he stepped forward, eyes locking with Astra's. "I have to do this."

Astra's eyes widened in horror. "No, Kael! There has to be another way! We've fought so hard, come so far… we can't lose you now!"

But Kael smiled, a sad, yet peaceful smile. "This is what I was meant for," he said quietly. "We all have a part to play in this battle. You were meant to lead. I was meant to protect—to sacrifice if need be. This… is my time."

Liora's hands trembled as tears filled her eyes. "We'll never forget you," she whispered, her voice breaking. "Your sacrifice will mean everything."

Draven's shadow flickered in the light, his expression dark and conflicted. "There's no going back from this, Kael," he warned, though his voice held a note of respect. "Are you certain?"

Kael nodded, his gaze steady. "I've never been more certain."

Zephyr, usually filled with bravado and jokes, stood silent for a moment, his eyes filled with something akin to sorrowful pride. "You're a true hero, Kael," he said quietly. "We'll finish this. You can count on that."

Ethan's equipment hummed softly as he adjusted it one final time, his voice heavy with emotion. "We'll make sure your sacrifice isn't in vain, Kael."

Kael stepped into the center of the group's protective circle, positioning himself at the heart of the artifacts. The power of the Eternal One swirled around him, growing in intensity as the light began to concentrate on his form. His sword, once a simple weapon of battle, now glowed with the divine energy of the artifacts. Kael closed his eyes, feeling the warmth of the Eternal One's presence surround him.

With one final look at his companions, Kael raised his sword high, and with a cry that echoed across the battlefield, he channeled the full power of the artifacts into a single, blinding explosion of light. The ground quaked beneath them as the radiant energy surged out from Kael, spreading across the battlefield in a wave of pure, unstoppable force.

Serath let out a final, anguished scream as the light consumed him, his dark form disintegrating under the force of the Eternal One's power. The shadows that had once clung to the battlefield were obliterated, and for the first time in what felt like an eternity, the world was bathed in the warm, golden glow of the Eternal One's light.

And when the light finally faded, Kael was gone.

SCENE 5 - YEAR 3127 - DAY 099: THE AFTERMATH

The battlefield was silent. The once tumultuous landscape was now still, the ground scorched and smoking in the wake of the final explosion of light. The creatures of darkness were gone, their twisted forms erased from existence, and with them, the threat of Serath had been vanquished.

But at what cost?

Astra stood at the center of it all, her staff lowered, her hand trembling as the weight of the loss settled over her. Kael was gone. The warrior who had stood beside her through every trial, every battle, had given everything to save the universe. Tears welled in her eyes, and she fell to her knees, her voice a quiet whisper carried on the wind. "Kael… we did it… but we lost you."

Draven's shadow magic flickered as he bowed his head in silent respect, his usually unreadable expression tinged with sorrow. "He was a true warrior," Draven said quietly. "A hero until the end."

Liora's healing light, always so bright, was dimmed with the weight of her grief. She knelt beside Astra, her hands trembling as tears streamed down her face. "He sacrificed himself for all of us," she whispered. "We'll never forget him."

Zephyr stood silent, his energy blaster lowered, his usual grin replaced with a solemn expression. "He was the best of us," Zephyr murmured. "We'll carry his memory with us, wherever we go."

Ethan adjusted his equipment one final time, the soft hum of his scanners barely audible in the heavy silence that followed. "We did it, Kael," he said softly, his voice thick with emotion. "We finished the fight. You saved us all."

As they stood in the quiet aftermath, a soft, golden light began to descend from the heavens. It was the light of the Eternal One, shining down upon the battlefield like a benediction. It bathed the world in warmth, a symbol of peace and hope that Kael's sacrifice had secured.

SCENE 6 - YEAR 3127 - DAY 100: THE RETURN TO LUMORA

The journey back to Lumora was quiet, filled with the weight of loss and the relief of victory. The land that had once been plagued by darkness was now bathed in the golden glow of the Eternal One's light. The twisted creatures that had once terrorized the world were no more, and the threat of Serath had been vanquished.

As they approached the gates of Lumora, they were greeted by a hero's welcome. The streets were lined with people, their faces filled with joy and gratitude. But the group's hearts were heavy, the loss of Kael still fresh in their minds.

Astra led the way, her staff glowing softly as they entered the city. The people of Lumora cheered and celebrated, but the group's thoughts were with their fallen comrade.

The council of Lumora awaited them in the city square, their expressions a mixture of pride and sorrow. "You have done well," the head of the council said, his voice filled with respect. "The universe is safe, thanks to your bravery and sacrifice."

Astra nodded; her voice quiet as she replied. "Kael… he gave everything to save us all. We couldn't have done it without him."

The council members bowed their heads in respect. "His sacrifice will not be forgotten," the head of the council said solemnly. "He will be remembered as a true hero."

As the group stood in the city square, surrounded by the people of Lumora, they reflected on the journey they had undertaken. They had saved the universe, but it had come at a great cost. They had lost a friend, a warrior, a hero. But they had succeeded.

And as they looked to the future, they knew that Kael's memory would live on in their hearts, a reminder of the strength and courage that had carried them through the darkest moments. They had answered the call to adventure, and they had emerged victorious.

With the light of the Eternal One guiding their way, they returned to Lumora, ready to face whatever the future might bring.

CHAPTER 14:

THE LIGHT THAT NEVER FADES

SCENE 1 - YEAR 3127 - DAY 101: A WORLD AWAKENED

THE FIRST LIGHT OF DAWN BROKE OVER THE HORIZON, CASTING A WARM, GOLDEN GLOW ACROSS THE LANDSCAPE OF LUMORA. THE CITY, ONCE SHROUDED IN THE SUFFOCATING SHADOW OF SERATH'S DARKNESS, NOW STOOD AS A BEACON OF HOPE AND RENEWAL. THE STREETS THRUMMED WITH THE SOUND OF CELEBRATION, THE VOICES OF THOSE WHO HAD LIVED UNDER FEAR AND OPPRESSION NOW RISING IN JOYFUL HARMONY. BANNERS FLUTTERED IN THE GENTLE BREEZE, ADORNED WITH THE COLORS OF FREEDOM, AND THE SCENT OF BLOOMING FLOWERS FILLED THE AIR, A TESTAMENT TO THE WORLD'S SLOW BUT STEADY HEALING.

From a high balcony overlooking the city, Astra stood alone, her eyes scanning the landscape below. The weight of the battle still clung to her like a shadow, though its grip had loosened with victory. Her staff rested by her side, glowing softly with the lingering power of the artifacts. Yet in this moment of triumph, a profound sense of loss gnawed at her. The battle was over. The universe was safe. But not all of them had made it through.

Kael's absence was a wound still raw, a hollow ache that no victory could soothe. His sacrifice, while noble, had carved a permanent scar in Astra's heart. She could almost see him now, standing beside her, his quiet strength a comfort she hadn't realized she'd leaned on so much. She closed her eyes, breathing deeply as the warmth of the dawn bathed her face. He is still with us, she reminded herself, his spirit woven into the light we fought to protect.

Footsteps sounded softly behind her, and Astra didn't need to turn to know who it was. Draven approached, his shadow magic a quiet whisper that danced around him, more serene now in the absence of Serath's darkness. The usual edge in his expression had softened, replaced by a rare moment of calm as he joined her at the balcony's edge.

"We've come a long way," Draven said quietly, his voice carrying a weight of reflection Astra hadn't heard in him before. "But it isn't over. There will always be shadows to fight, new dangers lurking in the places we cannot yet see. But for now, we've won."

Astra nodded, though the tension in her shoulders did not entirely ease. "We've won, but at what cost?" she murmured, her gaze drifting to the horizon. "Kael is gone. His sacrifice gave us this peace, but… it doesn't feel whole without him."

Liora's presence followed soon after, her healing light always a comforting balm to the spirit. She stepped beside Astra, her eyes following the same path as hers. "The people are free," she said softly, her voice imbued with the compassion that had carried them through so many trials. "They can live in peace now, something many thought impossible. That's what Kael wanted, Astra. We fought so they could live in the light, not in fear."

Astra swallowed hard, feeling the prick of tears. She did not let them fall. "I know," she whispered, "but it still feels like we've lost so much."

The sound of Zephyr's familiar laughter broke through the solemn atmosphere. He leaned against the balcony railing with a wide grin, the glint of mischief back in his eyes. "We saved the universe!" he declared; his voice filled with pride. "Not a bad day's work, if you ask me.

We've fought, we've bled, but look at us now. Serath's gone, the shadows are scattering, and the sun's shining again. If that's not victory, I don't know what is."

Ethan stood just behind him, adjusting his ever-buzzing equipment, though even his sharp, analytical mind seemed quieter today. He glanced at Astra; his brow furrowed in deep thought. "We've ensured the safety of the universe," he said, though his tone remained cautious. "But we can't rest on that alone. There's always more to learn, more to protect. If we let our guard down..."

Astra sighed, letting her gaze sweep over the city one more time before turning to face her companions fully. "I know," she said softly. "We've faced darkness, danger, and loss, and we've come out stronger on the other side. But our work isn't finished. There will always be new challenges, new threats to the light. We've been blessed with this victory, but we can't grow complacent."

Draven crossed his arms, his eyes narrowing slightly. "You sound just like Kael. Always thinking two steps ahead."

Astra smiled at the comparison, though her heart clenched at the thought of Kael's absence. "Kael knew what we all do. That our journey doesn't end with one victory. It continues."

They stood together, watching as the light of the sun slowly bathed Lumora in warmth and life. The battle was over, but as the dawn broke, it signaled not just the end of a war, but the beginning of a new era—one where the guardians of the light would always be called upon to protect the universe from the shadows that lurked just beyond the horizon.

The group's bond was stronger than ever, forged in the fires of battle and tempered by loss. Whatever lay ahead, they would face it together, just as they always had.

SCENE 2 - YEAR 3127 - DAY 101: THE ETERNAL ONE'S GIFT

As the morning light brightened, filling Lumora with the glow of a new day, Astra felt a familiar warmth envelop her, more profound than the rays of the rising sun. It was the presence of the Eternal One—a force that transcended time, space, and all that had been. She closed her eyes, surrendering to the gentle, yet overwhelming sensation of light filling her mind, her heart, her very soul.

In the quiet of her consciousness, Astra saw a vision unfold. The Eternal One stood before her, a being made of pure, radiant light, brighter than any sun, yet gentle and comforting. Around this magnificent figure was the endless expanse of the universe—a tapestry woven with stars, galaxies, and the boundless potential of life itself. There was no mistaking the Eternal One's presence, for it filled Astra with peace and a sense of belonging that was both humbling and exalting.

The Eternal One's voice resonated, not in her ears, but within her soul—a voice of infinite compassion, wisdom, and power. "You have done well, Astra," the Eternal One said, the words echoing like a soft melody. "You and your companions have saved the universe from darkness, and for that, you have my eternal gratitude. You have proven yourselves to be the protectors of the light."

Astra trembled, overwhelmed by the weight of those words. She felt unworthy of such praise. Her eyes remained closed, though tears formed beneath her lashes, not of sorrow, but of awe. "We only did what we had to," she whispered, her voice filled with reverence. "We fought to protect the light. To save the universe."

The Eternal One's light grew even brighter, its warmth wrapping around her like the embrace of a parent. "Your journey is far from over, Astra. The light must always be protected, for there will always be those who seek to extinguish it. But you and your companions have proven yourselves worthy. From this moment, you are the guardians of the universe, and I bless you with new powers and responsibilities to carry out this mission."

A surge of energy pulsed through Astra, more powerful than anything she had felt during the battle. Her body felt lighter, stronger, as if the very essence of the universe now flowed through her. It was not just her—it was her companions as well. She could sense it, the same surge of power filling each of them, transforming them in ways they had never imagined. The Eternal One was granting them more than just strength—it was granting them purpose.

In her mind's eye, Astra saw the artifacts glowing brighter than ever, merging their light into one unified force. The power of these ancient relics was no longer just a tool for battle—it was a guiding force that now belonged to them. Astra knew, in her heart, that this was the Eternal One's blessing manifest.

"You are now the Guardians of the Light," the Eternal One continued, its voice as soothing as it was empowering. "With this blessing comes great responsibility. You must remain vigilant, for the forces of darkness will always seek to return. But you are not alone. You have each other, and you have the light of the Eternal One to guide you always."

The vision faded, but the warmth remained. Astra opened her eyes to find herself once more on the balcony of Lumora, her heart still resonating with the power and wisdom of the Eternal One's message. She turned to her companions, who stood nearby, their faces a mixture of awe and wonder. They, too, had felt it—the blessing, the transformation. It was in the way Draven stood taller, his shadow magic now tempered with an even deeper sense of purpose. It was in the way Liora's healing light radiated with a soft, steady glow, more potent than before. Zephyr's usual bravado was replaced by a quiet, resolute confidence, and Ethan's keen mind buzzed with the possibilities their new powers might bring.

"We've been blessed by the Eternal One," Astra said, her voice barely more than a whisper, but the weight of her words was immense. "We've been given new powers, new responsibilities. We're the guardians of the universe now."

Draven was the first to speak, his voice a low rumble. "Guardians of the universe," he repeated, as if testing the weight of the title. "That's no small task."

Liora stepped forward, her healing light shimmering as she placed a gentle hand on Astra's arm. "We've always been protectors," she said softly, "but now... we're something more. Something greater. We've been entrusted with the future."

Zephyr, ever the optimist, grinned. "Well, I always knew we were special," he said, though there was no arrogance in his tone, only a quiet acknowledgment of the responsibility they had just inherited. "Looks like the universe has big plans for us."

Ethan adjusted the settings on his equipment, though his mind was clearly elsewhere. "This changes everything," he mused, his voice thoughtful. "We've been given a gift, a blessing. But it's also a challenge. We have to be ready for what's coming."

Astra's heart swelled with gratitude as she looked at her companions. Kael's absence still weighed heavily on them all, but in this moment, she knew he was with them—his spirit entwined in the light they had sworn to protect. They had lost much, but they had also gained something far greater: a purpose that transcended their personal struggles. Together, they had faced unimaginable darkness, and now they stood, blessed by the Eternal One, as the universe's final defense against those who would seek to destroy the light.

The dawn continued to rise, but for Astra and her companions, a new era had already begun.

SCENE 3 - YEAR 3127 - DAY 102: THE CROSSROADS

The sun climbed higher in the sky, casting its golden light across the bustling streets of Lumora. It was a day of celebration—of victory, of peace, and of hope restored. Yet, amidst the joy, there was a quiet undercurrent of bittersweet anticipation. The time had come for Astra and her companions to part ways, to embark on new journeys now that their grand mission had come to a close.

Astra stood at the gates of Lumora, her staff glowing faintly by her side. The weight of the coming farewell pressed against her chest, a dull ache that she could not shake. They had been through so much together—facing unimaginable darkness, sharing triumphs and losses, forging bonds that felt as eternal as the light they now swore to protect. And yet, the path ahead was one they each needed to walk alone.

Draven approached first, his presence as quiet and mysterious as ever, his shadow magic swirling subtly around him. He extended his hand, and Astra clasped it, feeling the warmth of his grip despite the shadows that surrounded him. "I'll always be there, in the shadows," Draven said, his voice low but steady. "If ever you need me, just call."

Astra smiled softly; her heart full of gratitude. "I know. Your strength has guided us through some of our darkest moments. We wouldn't have made it without you."

Draven's expression softened for a moment before the shadows seemed to close in around him once more. With a final nod, he stepped back, retreating into the cool shade of a nearby archway, as if already preparing for his next journey.

Liora was next, her healing light shining brightly as she approached Astra. Her eyes shimmered with unshed tears, her hands trembling as she reached out to embrace her friend. "I'll miss you all so much," she whispered, her voice thick with emotion. "We've shared so much… fought so hard together. But I know we'll meet again."

Astra hugged her tightly, blinking back her own tears. "You've been our beacon of hope, Liora. Your healing light has kept us going, even when the weight of the world was too much. I don't know what we'd have done without you."

Liora smiled through her tears, her light casting a soft glow around them both. "We're all part of the light now," she said quietly. "And that will always keep us connected, no matter where we are."

Zephyr's entrance was as lighthearted as ever, though Astra could sense the emotion hidden behind his usual grin. He clapped Astra on the shoulder, his energy infectious even in this moment of parting. "Well, look at us," he said, laughing softly. "We saved the universe, and now we're off to save a bit more of it. Not bad for a bunch of misfits, huh?"

Astra chuckled, shaking her head. "Not bad at all, Zephyr. Your optimism kept us going when things got rough. You always made sure we remembered why we were fighting."

Zephyr's grin softened. "And we'll keep fighting, right? No matter where we are, no matter what we face, we'll keep fighting for the light. I'll see you again, Astra. Count on it."

He stepped back, his usual swagger in his step, though Astra could see the weight of the goodbye in his eyes. Zephyr might have been the group's source of levity, but beneath the jokes and bravado, he had always cared deeply for them all.

Finally, Ethan approached, his mind as ever turning with the possibilities that lay ahead. He adjusted his equipment one last time before looking at Astra, his analytical mind temporarily set aside in favor of something more personal. "We've got new responsibilities now," he said thoughtfully, his voice softer than usual. "We'll be protecting the universe in ways we never imagined. But… we're still a team. We'll always be connected, no matter where we are."

Astra nodded, smiling. "You were our strategist, Ethan. Your mind saw paths the rest of us couldn't. We wouldn't have succeeded without you."

Ethan looked down for a moment, as if the compliment was too much to take in. Then, he smiled—genuine and sincere. "I'll miss you, Astra. But we've got work to do. We'll see each other again when the universe needs us."

The finality of the moment settled over the group like a soft, gentle mist. They shared one last embrace, each holding on for a moment longer than necessary, reluctant to let go. They had fought side by side, facing the greatest evil the universe had ever known. They had saved each other's lives, time and again. And now, they were saying goodbye.

As Astra stepped back, she looked into each of their faces, her heart full of both sadness and pride. "This isn't the end," she said softly, her voice thick with emotion. "We'll meet again. I'm sure of it. But for now, we each have our own paths to follow. And I know we'll do the Eternal One proud."

With those words, the group slowly began to part. Draven faded into the shadows, his form blending into the dark corners of the city. Liora, her light a constant companion, moved toward the temple where her healing gifts were needed. Zephyr, ever the adventurer, set off toward the horizon, his grin already returning as he planned his next escapade. Ethan lingered for a moment, adjusting his equipment one last time before heading off to continue his work as protector and strategist.

Astra remained at the gates of Lumora, watching her companions disappear into the distance. The city behind her was filled with light and laughter, the people celebrating their hard-won freedom. But here, at the edge of the city, she felt the quiet solitude of leadership, the burden of knowing that her journey was far from over.

She turned to look at the road ahead, knowing that new challenges awaited. But for now, she allowed herself a moment of peace, a moment to honor the journey they had all shared. She would miss them—her companions, her friends. But she knew, deep in her heart, that their paths would cross again.

With one final glance toward the horizon, Astra whispered a silent prayer to the Eternal One, asking for guidance, strength, and hope. Then, with her staff glowing softly by her side, she set off on her new journey, her heart filled with purpose and light.

SCENE 4 - YEAR 3127 - DAY 102: SHADOWS STIR

As the sun climbed higher into the sky, its rays bathed the land of Lumora in a warm, golden glow. The vibrant city streets teemed with life, the people reveling in their newfound freedom, their laughter and songs rising into the clear air. But beyond the city gates, Astra walked alone on a path that led toward the open world—a world that had been saved, but one that still held mysteries and shadows yet to be uncovered.

The morning was peaceful, the calm after the storm of battle. It was a silence that seemed to stretch into eternity, as if the universe itself was breathing a sigh of relief. But Astra knew better. She knew that peace, though hard-earned, was always fragile. The light needed to be guarded, tended to, and watched over. She had learned that lesson well.

Her staff glowed faintly in her hand, the relics of their journey still brimming with power. They had vanquished Serath and his darkness, but the road ahead would not always be so clear. There would be other forces, other enemies, who sought to plunge the universe back into chaos. The light of the Eternal One had to be protected, and it was now her duty—and the duty of her companions—to ensure that it always shone brightly.

Astra paused as she reached the crest of a hill, turning to look back at the city of Lumora one last time. The towers gleamed in the sunlight, their white stone walls reflecting the brilliance of the new day. It was a city reborn, a place where hope had triumphed over despair. But as beautiful as it was, she knew her place was out there, beyond the safety of its walls.

A familiar warmth filled her heart, and she closed her eyes as the presence of the Eternal One reached out to her once again. The connection was stronger now, deeper, as if the light itself had become a part of her.

The Eternal One's voice echoed softly in her mind, filling her with both peace and purpose.

"The light is eternal, Astra," the voice said, gentle yet firm. "And so is your mission. You and your companions are the guardians of this universe, and while peace has been won today, the darkness will always seek to return. You must remain vigilant, for the shadows never truly disappear."

Astra's grip on her staff tightened. She knew that truth all too well. But she also knew that the strength they had gained, the bond they had forged, would carry them through whatever came next.

"Go forth," the Eternal One's voice continued, "and remember that you are never alone. The light will always guide you, and your companions will always stand by your side, even when they are far away. Together, you are the light that pushes back the darkness."

Astra opened her eyes, the light of the Eternal One fading from her mind but leaving behind a renewed sense of purpose. She turned her gaze back to the horizon, the wide expanse of the world stretching out before her. Somewhere out there, new adventures awaited—new battles, new challenges, and perhaps even new allies. The universe was vast, and it was calling.

She took a deep breath, feeling the weight of her responsibility, but also the thrill of the unknown. This wasn't the end. It was merely the beginning of a new chapter—a new journey that would take her and her companions even further into the heart of the universe's mysteries.

Far behind her, in the distance, she could still sense them—Draven, Liora, Zephyr, and Ethan. Each of them had set off on their own paths, but they were never truly apart. The bond they had forged during their trials was unbreakable, and she knew that if ever the need arose, they would come together again.

With the city of Lumora behind her and the future stretching out before her, Astra stepped forward. The warmth of the sun kissed her skin, and the light of the Eternal One filled her heart. She was no longer just a warrior, no longer just a traveler seeking answers. She was a guardian of the universe, a protector of the light.

And so, with a determined heart and a quiet smile, Astra began her new journey. She walked into the light, the promise of endless possibilities ahead of her, and the knowledge that she—and her companions—would always be ready to defend the universe from whatever darkness dared to rise again.

As she walked, the final rays of sunlight bathed the land in a golden glow, and somewhere in the distance, she could feel the presence of her friends—her family.

They were out there, protecting the light in their own ways, each of them a beacon of hope for the universe.

The light of the Eternal One continued to shine, a beacon of strength, courage, and hope. And though the journey had reached its conclusion for now, Astra knew that their story was far from over.

The universe would always need guardians. And they would always be ready.

And thus, the first volume of their tale comes to an end, but the seeds of a greater story have been sown. The shadows may always return, but so too will the light, and with it, the heroes who will rise to meet it.

For now, the universe was at peace, but Astra and her companions were always ready, waiting for the call to arms—the call to protect the Eternal Light.

The end... for now.

EPILOGUE: THE AFTERMATH

SCENE 1 - YEAR 3127 - DAY 102: THE WORLD REBORN

IN THE AFTERMATH OF THE FINAL BATTLE, THE LANDSCAPE THAT HAD ONCE BEEN MARRED BY CHAOS NOW PULSED WITH NEW LIFE. THE FIELDS, ONCE RAVAGED BY WAR AND SHROUDED IN SHADOW, BLOOMED WITH WILDFLOWERS IN VIBRANT COLORS— PURPLES, REDS, YELLOWS—SYMBOLIZING THE REBIRTH OF THE WORLD. THE GOLDEN LIGHT OF THE ETERNAL ONE WARMED THE EARTH, COAXING LIFE FROM THE SCARS LEFT BY SERATH'S DARK FORCES. IT WAS AS THOUGH THE UNIVERSE ITSELF SOUGHT TO HEAL, EAGER TO CAST OFF THE REMNANTS OF DARKNESS.

Astra stood at the edge of the meadow, her heart swelling with both pride and sadness. The wind gently tousled her hair as she gazed upon the world they had fought to save. The people of Lumora, once burdened by fear and despair, moved about with a sense of hope. Laughter echoed from the city walls, children's voices rising with joy as they played in streets that had known the silence of war for far too long.

But despite the beauty of the scene before her, Astra's thoughts drifted to Kael. His absence lingered like a shadow in her heart. She felt the weight of his sacrifice with every step she took on the soil he had died to protect. His memory would forever be intertwined with this world's rebirth. His name would be remembered in every new flower that bloomed and in every joyful laugh that filled the air.

Draven approached silently from behind, his footsteps barely making a sound as he joined Astra at the edge of the meadow. "A world reborn," he murmured, his gaze scanning the horizon. "But as we both know, peace is fragile. Shadows will always linger at the edges, waiting for their moment."

Astra nodded; her voice soft but resolute. "We've won this battle, but the war against darkness never truly ends. There will always be more to protect."

Draven's eyes flickered with a rare moment of emotion, a deep understanding in his gaze. "But we'll be ready. Just as we always have been."

The two stood in silence, watching as the golden light of the Eternal One bathed the land in warmth. It was a world reborn, but also one in need of guardians—guardians who would stand vigilant, ready to defend it at a moment's notice.

SCENE 2 - YEAR 3127 - DAY 102: MONUMENT TO HEROES

In the heart of Lumora, where the city's greatest celebrations and sorrows were shared, stood a newly erected monument. Carved from gleaming white stone, it towered over the square, its surface adorned with the names of the fallen heroes. At its peak, a crystal orb reflected the sunlight, casting rainbows across the cobbled streets below.

The people of Lumora gathered in silence, offering prayers and laying flowers at the base of the monument. It was a time of mourning, but also a time of remembrance—of honoring those who had given everything to protect the light. Among the names etched into the stone was that of Kael.

Astra stood at the monument, her fingers brushing over the letters of Kael's name. She could still see his face clearly in her mind—the fierce determination in his eyes, the unwavering courage with which he had faced the darkness. Her heart ached, but she felt a quiet pride in knowing that his sacrifice had not been in vain.

"He would've hated this," Zephyr said, his usual grin tinged with sadness as he joined her. "Kael wasn't one for monuments. He'd have said something like, 'I did what had to be done.' But this…" He gestured to the shining orb above. "This is for us, to remember."

Liora's healing light shimmered softly beside them as she spoke, her voice filled with reverence. "Kael gave us a future. We owe it to him to live it well."

The group stood in silent unity, each lost in their own memories. The monument wasn't just a symbol of loss, but of hope—hope that the sacrifices made had given the universe a chance at peace. And though the names of the fallen would forever be carved in stone, their legacy lived on in the light of the Eternal One, shining brightly for all to see.

SCENE 3 - YEAR 3127 - DAY 103: THE ETERNAL ONE'S LEGACY

Later that night, Astra found herself once again drawn to the temple of the Eternal One. It was a place of quiet reflection, where the Eternal Flame burned eternally, symbolizing the unending light that guided the universe.

The temple's interior was peaceful, the flickering flames casting warm shadows across the stone walls. Astra knelt before the Eternal Flame; her mind filled with thoughts of the journey that had led her here. She had faced darkness and despair, lost friends, and witnessed the weight of sacrifice. But through it all, the light had remained. And it had grown stronger, not just within the world, but within her.

The voice of the Eternal One echoed softly in her mind, as it had many times before. "Astra, you have carried the light through the darkest of times. But know this—your journey is not yet over. Darkness will always seek to return, but as long as you and your companions remain vigilant, the light will never fade."

Astra bowed her head, feeling the weight of those words settle within her. "I know," she whispered. "I know the darkness isn't gone forever. But we'll be ready. I'll be ready."

The Eternal Flame flickered, as if acknowledging her words. "You have been granted strength and wisdom, Astra. You are the light's guardian, now and always."

As Astra rose to her feet, she felt a renewed sense of purpose, a quiet resolve that burned within her like the Eternal Flame itself. Her journey was far from over, but she no longer feared the darkness. She had her companions, her strength, and the light of the Eternal One to guide her.

SCENE 4 - YEAR 3127 - DAY 105:
THE LIGHT OF THE FUTURE

On the final day of their stay in Lumora, the group gathered one last time, standing at the edge of the city where the horizon stretched out before them. The sun was setting, casting the sky in shades of pink and gold. The light of the Eternal One shimmered faintly in the distance, a reminder of the path they had chosen to walk.

Astra turned to her companions; her heart full. "This isn't the end," she said softly, her voice steady. "There will always be darkness to fight, and the light will always need protectors. We've come so far, but our journey is far from over."

Draven nodded, his expression calm and resolute. "The shadows may return, but they'll find us waiting."

Liora smiled gently, her healing light glowing softly. "We've faced so much together, and we'll face whatever comes next."

Zephyr grinned, the sparkle in his eyes returning. "And we'll kick its butt, just like always."

Ethan adjusted his equipment, a familiar hum of energy surrounding him. "We've gathered the tools, the knowledge, and the strength. We'll always be ready."

As the last rays of sunlight dipped below the horizon, Astra took a deep breath, feeling the warmth of the Eternal One's light on her skin. The future stretched out before them, uncertain and full of possibilities, but they were ready.

The light of the Eternal One would guide them, always. And no matter what challenges lay ahead, they would face them together, united in purpose, bound by the strength of their bond.

For now, the universe was at peace. But Astra and her companions knew that their true mission was just beginning. The light had been saved, but it would need to be protected for all time.

With the light of the Eternal One glowing within them, they stepped forward into the future—guardians of the universe, defenders of hope, and protectors of the light.

And so, their story continued…

ACKNOWLEDGEMENTS

This book would not be what it is today without the incredible support and insights of my beta readers. Your encouragement, feedback, and thoughtful observations helped transform this story into something greater than I could have envisioned on my own.

To Bill Pennifield, Michael Bass, James Burke, and Jacob Pignaloso: Your dedication, patience, and honest critiques were invaluable in shaping this manuscript. Each of you brought unique perspectives that allowed me to see the story in new ways, improving it beyond what I initially imagined.

To all my beta readers, your enthusiasm kept me going. Whether it was pointing out areas for improvement, challenging my ideas, or simply offering words of encouragement, your input was essential every step of the way.

Finally, to my loving wife—your unwavering support and encouragement have been my anchor throughout this journey. From listening to my ideas to pushing me forward when I needed it most, your belief in me made all the difference. This book exists in part because of you.

To all of you, this book is as much yours as it is mine. Thank you for being an essential part of this journey. I am profoundly grateful to each and every one of you.

COMING SOON IN THE ETERNAL HORIZONS SERIES

Book 2: The Shattered Realms

In the aftermath of their first quest, Astra and her companions must navigate a fractured universe where the lines between light and darkness blur. Old allies return, new enemies emerge, and the stakes have never been higher.

Book 3: The Shadow's Embrace

As the darkness tightens its grip, the guardians face their greatest fears in the Shadow Realm. Secrets long buried come to light, and the fate of the universe hangs in the balance.

Book 4: The Eternal War

The forces of light and darkness collide in an epic battle for control of the universe. Friendships will be tested, sacrifices will be made, and the true power of the Eternal One will be revealed.

Book 5: The Final Ascension

In the climactic conclusion of the Eternal Horizons Series, Astra and her companions embark on their final journey to restore balance to the universe. The end is near, but the outcome remains uncertain. Will they rise above the darkness, or will the universe be plunged into eternal night?

Stay tuned for these upcoming adventures!